A line of Indians came over the rise, charging at Longarm and Bonnie in the moonlight.

Longarm grabbed the redhead and swung her in place, with the pistol aimed across the buckskin to the north as he covered them from the rear with the Winchester . . .

"You've only got four rounds in that gun now, Red. Do you know how to reload a revolver?"

"Of course. Don't fuss at me. Give me the damned bullets!"

He laughed, reached in his coat pocket, and handed her some loose rounds. "Hang on to these. You're all right, Red. We might just get out of this with our hair yet."

—◆— TABOR EVANS —◆—

AND THE
BLACKFOOT GUNS

A JOVE BOOK

LONGARM AND THE BLACKFOOT GUNS

A Jove Book/published by arrangement with
the author

PRINTING HISTORY
Jove editon/May 1985

ISBN: 0-515-08190-6

Chapter 1

Stretch O'Hanlon felt taller than most men when he was wearing his guns. But he wasn't wearing his guns when they shoved him into a patent cell at the Denver Federal House of Detention and, without his guns and despite his humorous nickname, young Stretch stood five foot four wearing three-inch Texas heels. When he saw who they were locking him in with he protested to the turnkey, "Can't I at least have my own private room for the night, damn it? There's plenty of empty cells in this dim deserted wing, you know."

The turnkey just slid the bars shut and locked him in with the giant watching bemused from the bottom bunk. The more sociable guard who'd helped escort the prisoner past one empty cell after another to the very end of the block laughed lightly and said, "There's no sense mopping two cells in the cold gray when there's plenty of room in one for both you boys. Don't be so unsociable, Stretch. I should think you'd enjoy the company. It ain't like either of you sons of bitches is likely to meet anybody more interesting than one another for a spell."

The considerably bigger occupant of the now ominously crowded cell sat up, swung his own big feet to the gritty cement floor, and laughed in a sort of spooky way. The guard sobered. "I don't want you bothering this kid, Shorty. I mean it," he said.

The big man on the bottom bunk grinned thoughtfully up at the now very nervous newcomer and said, "Shoot,

1

Dutch, I ain't been locked up that long. Any word from my lawyer?"

The guard shook his head. "Since he don't know we have you yet, you can forget about him and your old pal, Habeas J. Corpus, this side of your arraignment, you sneaky bastard. How many times did you really expect us to let you pull that same old chestnut on the Justice Department, Shorty?"

The man on the bunk shrugged. "Many times as I have to, I reckon," he said. "I don't enjoy the federal pens worth a damn."

The lawmen on the more comfortable side of the bars told both of the men in the cell to behave and headed back to the wardroom to finish their card game. As their boot heels echoed down the hall the man they'd dubbed Shorty because he was so big gazed fondly up at the nervous prisoner who was called Stretch because he was so short and said, "Well, little darling, I sure hope you thought to bring along a deck of cards or at least a pair of dice. For it can't be later than seven or eight outside and we got us one long tedious night to kill afore the infernal judge gets to work in the morning."

Stretch O'Hanlon gulped and said, "The sons of bitches didn't even leave me my tobacco. I guess I get the top bunk, right?"

His big cellmate rose from the bunk. "Hell, little darling, you just lay your head upon the bottom pillow all you like as you cries yourself to sleep," he said. "I don't figure on spending the whole night here."

He strode over to the boiler-plate rear wall and rapped it with his big knuckles thoughtfully, making it ring like a dull gong as he mused aloud, "Modern science sure is a caution, ain't it? But it'll take more'n a patent cell to hold *me* all that long. What are you in for, little darling? Purse snatching?"

2

Stretch O'Hanlon drew himself to his full modest height as he protested with indignation, "I ain't nobody's little darling, damn it! I'm a full-growed railroad plunderer and if I had my guns handy I could show you enough notches on the grips to command a little respect around here!"

His taller cellmate smiled down at him indulgently. "You don't have to scare me, little darling. Like I said, I don't mean to spend the whole night here. But if you want some fatherly advice about your coming debut at Leavenworth, don't try to pull that big bad bullshit on the hardcase lifers you'll be meeting there. Just butter up to the bully of your cellblock and, once you're his, nobody else will bother you, see?"

Stretch O'Hanlon gasped, looked like he was about to be sick, then managed not to, just, as he protested, "You're talking crazy! I ain't that kind of a gent, God damn it!"

The bigger and obviously more mature Shorty reached inside his dark brown frock coat as he nodded and said, "I didn't think you'd ever done heavy time afore, little darling. But don't worry your pretty little head about it. Time you get out of Leavenworth you may even *enjoy* it."

Then he took out two cheroots and a kitchen match, adding, "I'd show you how if I figured to spend that much time with you, little darling. But, like I said, my lawyer will be coming to spring me long afore I could work up a passion for anyone as ugly as you. So have a smoke and let's change the subject."

The young train robber accepted the smoke. But as his big cellmate thumbed a light for both of them he frowned and asked, "How come they let you keep your tobacco? They took mine away, damn it."

Shorty shook out the light and moved back over to the bunks as he said disdainfully, "It's obvious as hell you ain't used to getting your fool self arrested. Who took your smokes, that morose turnkey they calls Smiley?"

The younger prisoner nodded. His cellmate sat on one end of the bottom bunk as he said, "Thought so. He ain't what one could call neighborly. I generally try and get that fatter and friendlier gent, Dutch, to pat me down. Old Dutch knows the facts of life. He takes that same gold eagle out of that same vest pocket ever' time, and we say no more about what I may or may not have in my other pockets."

He blew a thoughtful smoke ring before adding wistfully, "Of course, there's limits to what even an understanding screw can allow. I doubt old Dutch would overlook a belly gun, a saw, or even a serious knife. But he knows I ain't an escape artist and, even if I was, how in hell would I go about carving my way out of a patent cell with the few comforts of home a neighborly screw is willing to overlook?"

There was nowhere else to sit up straight, since the top bunk was within eighteen inches of the boiler-plate ceiling, so Stretch sat gingerly down at the far end of the bottom bunk. "I can see you've passed this way afore, Shorty," he observed. "Mind if I ask you what they have on you this time?"

The taller man frowned ominously at him, blew smoke out his nostrils like a bull about to charge, then relaxed. "I can see you're green as grass. So I'll tell you again, fatherly, a new fish is supposed to keep his mouth shut about a senior con's business, unless or until the older con wants to tell him about it. You ain't in Leavenworth yet. When you get there, don't ask nobody what they're in for. It's the sure sign of either a new fish or a con serving so much time he don't give a shit no more. Most of the boys you'll meet are still hoping to get out on appeal, and it's hard as hell to convince the law they have the wrong man after you've blabbed your life story to a stool pigeon!"

He frowned again, harder this time, and growled, "Come to think on it, that sneaky Billy Vail would do anything to get the goods on me and, come to think on it even harder, I never heard of *you* Stretch O'Hanlon! Are you sure old Billy Vail didn't lock you in with me as a ruse?"

Stretch paled. "That's just stupid, Shorty! You heard me tell 'em I didn't even want to be locked up with you! As for this Vail gent you has me in cahoots with, I never heard of the son of a bitch! Who's he supposed to be, Shorty?"

There was a long, ominous silence before the tall man at the far end of the bunk asked flatly, "Who picked you up, if it wasn't Marshal Vail in the flesh?"

"Vail's a marshal? I swear I never heard of him until just now. I was nailed in the Union Depot late this afternoon by a deputy calt Guilfoyle. He throwed down at me in the gents' room as I was taking a leak, the sneaky bastard. Had I spotted him first . . ."

"Yeah, yeah, you're a big bad owlhoot as can do wonders and eat cucumbers," the other man cut in with a disdainful expression. "Anyone working for the law here in Denver would know the names of Vail's deputies. But let's not worry about it, little darling. Like I said, I don't figure on staying here long enough to spill anything they could really hold me on, even in my sleep."

Stretch stared thoughtfully at the empty corridor beyond the bars as he observed, "That one calt Dutch said your lawyer wasn't aware of your present situation, and didn't you say he was the *friendly* one?"

His cellmate leaned back against the boiler plate, took a drag on his cheroot, and chuckled fondly as he answered, "I'll bet you all my smokes that I'm out of here before midnight."

"I reckon I'll sure win me some tobacco," O'Hanlon replied, "for I don't see how in hell you figures to get out of here afore they comes for us both in the morning, Shorty."

His misnamed cellmate shrugged and said, "Maybe my lawyer knows where I am and maybe he don't. I told you your boss, Billy Vail, is a slick old devil, but I'm slick, too. So I'm betting the marshals will *tell* my lawyer they've arrested me, if not by midnight, at least before they have to take me before a hung-over judge with such a ridiculous charge. You know, of course, there's no way in hell to make statutory rape stick in a federal court, don't you, little darling?"

Stretch winced. "I sure wish you wouldn't call me that. I had no idea what they was holding you on until just now, but I has to agree the notion of raping a statue sounds mighty silly."

The bigger man laughed loudly. "By Jesus, I don't think you *could* be one of old Vail's sissy lawmen after all, unless you got a mighty sardonic sense of humor. Statutory rape, you idjet, is the screwing of a she-male under the age of consent, whether she's willing or not."

"Oh, then you never raped a statue or anybody else, right?"

"Hell, no, I'm too good-looking to have to wrestle for my love life. The law found out I was keeping company with a . . . well, sort of young gal. So, not having anything sensible to charge me with, they arrested me on statutory rape. Ain't that a bitch?"

"I've heard tell a gent could get in a fix like that with young gals. Uh . . . how young *was* this sporting gal of yourn, Shorty?"

"Ain't sure. Fifteen, sixteen, something like that. Women always lie about their age, you know."

Little Stretch began to feel taller as he stared in growing disgust at his big rawboned cellmate. "You don't need no lawyer, Shorty. You needs a doc to examine your head!

6

How could any man with a lick of sense trifle with a bitty gal of that age? It's no wonder they arrested you! I thought *I* was in trouble, but I wouldn't trade places with you afore any judge and jury now. You're going to get the book throwed at you, Shorty! I've heard tell of men catching twenty at hard for messing with fifteen-year-olds."

His big cellmate laughed easily and said, "A lot you know. In the first damn place, this here's a federal cell, and any kind of rape is a local offense unless it takes place on a military or Indian reservation. In the second plase, the gal ain't fixing to testify against me. She was willing, I tell you, so I broke her in."

"I don't care if you're bigger than me. You're disgusting."

"Flattery will get you nowhere, little darling. I don't see what's disgusting about breaking in a she-male right. Sooner or later all the men and women has to be separated from the boys and gals, when you get right down to it. I've always been grateful as hell to the older neighbor gal as showed me what my kid hard-ons was really good for."

Stretch O'Hanlon calmed down a bit but shook his head and said, "I could never mistreat kids like that. I've done some awful things, I reckon, but I was raised by gentlefolk to treat women and children decent."

The big man on the bunk blew a smoke ring and taunted, "That's why you're on your way to Leavenworth for at least twenty years and I'll be going home. No offense, Stretch, but your folks raised you wrong."

Before O'Hanlon could answer, they both heard footsteps out in the corridor. The taller man rose to join the shorter at the bars as a stubby gent in a business suit, older by far than either man in the cell and midway between them in size, stopped at the cell door to growl in a disgusted voice, "I just got word an hour ago. I've been spending most of

7

the time since listening to disgusting tales about you, Shorty. How in the hell could you have lowered yourself to fooling with a kid?"

"You got my habeas corpus from our friendly neighborhood judge yet?" Shorty asked, ignoring his lawyer's question.

The older, stubbier man outside the cell grimaced and said, "Yes and no. I don't want to serve it until a certain local judge who's on friendlier terms with the federal prosecutor leaves town on the night train for a political meeting down in Colorado Springs. It's true they can't hold you on child molesting, federal, but we'd look pretty dumb if I was to spring you from this frying pan into the fire, old son. Let the judge we can't fix get sort of out of reach and—"

"Damn it, counselor!" his client cut in. "I just bet this punk all my tobacco I'd be outten here by midnight!"

The older and apparently wiser visitor snorted. "I will have you out by midnight," he said. "Meanwhile, I have to make sure the local police don't arrest you two minutes later. So behave yourself and I'll get back to you as soon as I can."

He turned to leave, but Stretch O'Hanlon said, "Hold it! Not so fast, damn it! If you can get this sex maniac out, you ought to be able to get *me* out, right?"

The older man stared through the bars at the young train robber as if he were staring through a microscope at a bug. He asked the taller man in the cell, "Friend of yours, Shorty?"

"Don't know," Shorty replied. "He says he's a well-knowed gunslick. I've never heard of him."

The visitor stared blankly through the bars and said, "Neither have I. You got any money, sonny? Like it says in the Good Book, money is the root, and prices are a scandal in a big town like Denver."

Stretch O'Hanlon gulped. "I don't even have my tobacco,

8

on me. But anyone can tell you my credit's good."

The older man smiled crookedly. "No, they can't. Nobody I know, personal, knows you. Who the hell are you supposed to be, and what are they holding you on?"

"I'm Stretch O'Hanlon. I was riding considerable with Hard-Ass Henry Harrison. Surely you've heard of him?"

"Not recent. As I heard it, Hard-Ass Henry slapped leather with an ugly-natured federal deputy called Longarm, up Dakota way a spell back. So Hard-Ass Henry ain't about to vouch for anyone, pilgrim. You ever hear of this young rascal's notorious sidekick, Shorty?"

The other man in the cell frowned thoughtfully and then said grudgingly, "I've seen the name on reward posters. May have even been in the same saloon with him at least once. Never got to know him. Didn't want to. He wasn't much. Just a cowboy gone wrong who got his fool self shot before he could amount to much."

"That's a lie!" protested O'Hanlon, adding in an angry tone, "Hard-Ass Henry was one of the best. I was with him when he stopped the U.P. Flier up in the south pass, and it went slick as silk! Hard-Ass Henry taught me all there is to know about the business."

The older man outside nodded sagely and said, "That's why you're on that side of the bars and I'm out here, right? You haven't told me what they've charged you with, sonny."

"They're only holding me on suspicion. Some infernal witnesses seem to put me up in the south pass with Hard-Ass Henry on an inconvenient date. But I don't see how they can prove it, do you?"

"Don't know. I know for a fact that Marshal Billy Vail is smart as hell. I can't see him locking either of you up with what the blotter out front says they're holding you on. I'll tell you what I'll do for you, sonny. You give me the name of someone here in town with the wherewithal to bail

9

you out, and we'll see what we shall see."

O'Hanlon sighed wistfully. "I don't have no friends in Denver. I was just passing through, in hopes of avoiding a discussion with the law further north."

The older man shrugged. "My heart bleeds for you. But I just can't reach you." He turned away, calling back as he left, "I should have *you* out in about an hour, Shorty."

Chapter 2

The big man called Shorty sat down again, examined his cheroot, and stubbed it out to light another as the smaller train robber sat down beside him, sobbing. "It ain't fair! All I've ever done is rob a few old trains and I gotta sit here whilst a goddam baby-raper goes free!"

His cellmate, who now seemed in a more jovial mood, for obvious reasons, said, "Don't cry, little darling. I'll leave you some smokes."

"You got to talk your lawyer into getting me out, too!" Stretch begged.

"How am I to manage that, little darling? He ain't getting *me* out because he *likes* me. I have to *pay* the son of a bitch every time we go through this. I may just have to move my base of operations if they keep pestering me like this here in Denver. But, what the hell, we've made as much in other parts before. Mebbe I'll take the gang to Salt Lake, next. Them Mormon lawmen don't get so excited about gents living with more'n one woman."

"I don't want to hear about your disgusting ways with she-males," O'Hanlon cut in. "Just what sort of lawbreaking are you in for *money,* damn it?"

"Did I say I was an outlaw? I don't know what ever gave you such a notion, little darling. I want it distinct on the record, should you turn out to have a stenographer taking all this down for the law, that I've told you from the start I ain't guilty of any infernal federal crime and that my being here at all is just a ruse on the part of that sneaky old Billy

11

Vail. So you can just tell your pards it didn't work. For I come in here innocent and I'm leaving innocent, as soon as that son of a bitch we just talked to gets back here with the damned old key!"

O'Hanlon said, "Bullshit. You can't fool me. Nobody has judges on such friendly negotiating terms unless he's a serious crook. Look here: I'm a serious crook, too, and you gotta help me."

"Why? You ain't got any money."

"Damn it, I can get some money, plenty of money, once I'm out of here! You're right about Hard-Ass Henry getting killed in a shootout just a few weeks after we stopped the U.P. Flier. He ran into that deputy up in Middle Fork before he could spend his share of the loot, see?"

"I don't see shit, little darling. Your sidekick's buried, with or without money in his jeans. I wasn't at the funeral. What happened to *your* share, if this job you pulled was so astoundingly profitsome?"

Stretch O'Hanlon looked sheepish. "Spent mostly on slow horses and fast women. I ain't in the business to *invest* money. I enjoy *spending* it! But you ain't paying attention. Hard-Ass Henry got the leader's share, and then he got kilt before he could spend enough of it to matter!"

His cellmate rolled his eyes heavenward, or at least up at the boiler plate above them, and said, "Oh, God, spare me tales of buried treasure! You know, I can find me a prospector in every saloon west of the Big Muddy who will sell me a treasure map for the price of a few drinks."

"I'm not talking about no infernal buried treasure, Shorty! I'm talking about close to ten thousand dollars in hard cash that Hard-Ass Henry had on him when he was kilt!"

The older, wiser-looking man shook his head. "Won't work. I read something about the shootout in the *Post,* now that I study on it. Your old boss was gunned down in a saloon by a federal agent, then buried at the expense of the town, in a pauper's grave. Don't you reckon *anyone* would have noticed the contents of the dead rascal's pockets at the time?"

"I read the papers, too! That's how I know the money was never recovered! So if you and your pards can get me out of here, I can just go up to Middle Fork and—"

"Sure you could!" the other cut in with an unkind laugh. "You must think I was behind the door when the brains was passed out, little darling. Even if we trusted your intentions, which we don't, how in thunder would you be able to recover a bankroll the late Hard-Ass Henry could have dropped most anyplace in his tangled travels after you'd all split up after the robbery?"

O'Hanlon chuckled and said, "Easy. I know why he rode to Middle Fork in the first place. He went to see a certain gal. A growed-up gal, no offense, with no-questions rooms to let and other charms Hard-Ass hankered for, to hear him tell it."

His cellmate blew another thoughtful smoke ring and shook his head. "That don't sound much better than any other treasure map I could buy a lot cheaper, little darling. It'd cost me real *dinero* to get you out of here. The only way I see that might work would be to go your bail and then let you skip bail. I doubt even my lawyer could bail you out for less than five thousand."

"So what? I told you Harrison had at least ten left when he died. I know where he was rooming in Middle Fork. I know he'd have never been so in love with a whore he'd have left it with *her!* So it has to be hid in the room he was sharing with her, see?"

"You mean under a floorboard or something? Hmm. What's the name of this sporting gal in Middle Fork?"

O'Hanlon laughed shrewdly. "You get me outten here

before we discuss any lady's reputation further, hear?"

The bigger man chuckled. "Yeah, I figured you were too smart to tell me. I'll talk it over with my own bunch later. If they see any advantage to getting you outten here, you'll get out. If they don't, you won't."

"I swear I can lead you right to the money!" O'Hanlon protested.

His cellmate rose, muttering, "Hold the thought. Someone's coming, and I don't like to talk business in front of screws."

As a matter of fact, it was the morose turnkey called Smiley, with Shorty's lawyer, this time grinning broadly as he called out, "All right, Shorty. You've spent enough time in there for now. Let's go."

Smiley opened the door. The tall man called Shorty stepped out. O'Hanlon didn't get to, of course. He wailed, "Don't forget, Shorty!" as they all wandered off to leave him alone, trying not to cry.

They didn't go as far as the young owlhoot assumed. The man who'd been in the cell and the man who'd got him out parted company with the turnkey at the far end of the corridor, then circled the cheek-by-jowl patent cells to follow another corridor to its own far end before they entered a cell separated from the one O'Hanlon was still locked up in by one thin sheet of boiler plate. Just in case the plates weren't thin enough, Marshal Billy Vail had thoughtfully had a rivet removed before anyone had been placed in the cell on the other side. A petite brunette with a shorthand pad in the lap of her poplin dress was still seated on a stool with her left ear near the listening hole and a maidenly blush on her pretty face.

Marshal Vail kept his voice low as he asked her, "Did you get it all, Miss Wiggins?"

She couldn't look at him. Deputy U. S. Marshal Custis

14

Long, alias Shorty, murmured, "More than she bargained for, I fear!"

"Did you *have* to talk so dirty, Longarm?" the young woman asked.

Longarm picked up his gun rig and Stetson from the cell bunk he'd left them on before assuming his identity as cellmate to the only real prisoner in the otherwise deserted wing of the detention house. He put them on as he whispered, "Let's get out of earshot so's we can talk less sneaky."

The three of them left, with the petite Miss Wiggins between the two men, clutching her pad primly to her starched bodice as she tried not to listen to them talking across her. Longarm had noticed the young gal's burning ears and was trying to keep it delicate, but his boss was gloating with glee as he said, "The punk thought he was so smart, trying to hold out on them few last loose ends. I'll bet had I left you in there with him another hour he'd have writ down the very name and address of that cathouse up to Middle Fork, Longarm!"

Longarm shook his head and said, "We was pushing our luck when I signaled you with that boot scrape to come and get me. I fear I rubbed the Constitution a mite raw for me ever to appear in court against the varmint, just getting him to admit the guilty knowledge we needed to hang him."

Miss Wiggins frowned between them as she tried to fathom their arcane conversation. But she was only a court stenographer, not a lawyer or even a lawman, so she didn't fully understand when Marshal Vail replied, "You're likely right. O'Hanlon can't get out of knowing the leader of his gang rode to Middle Fork and why. But actually recovering part of that railroad money would cheer the federal prosecutor as well as the Union Pacific no end. Who did you say that Dakota lawman you worked with so good a spell back was?"

Longarm replied, "Lansford. He calls himself Sheriff

15

Lansford, even if it is an unincorporated county. I found him a decent old cuss despite his casual attitude on election procedures. Naturally you want me to wire him to dig up the *dinero*, right?"

Vail nodded, then thought harder and said, "No. I'd better tend to it myself, lest your tainted name appear on the resulting legal corespondings. As of now you're off the case and I'll be switched if I know just who the cellmate O'Hanlon was jawing so freely with might have been."

Longarm chuckled and said, "Great minds run in the same ditching. Can I go home now, boss?"

"Not yet. And don't get the notion this overtime entitles you to show up at the office even later than usual in the morning," Vail said. "I'll go wire Sheriff Lansford. You see Miss Wiggins, here, back to the federal building. It's almost eleven and that's too late for an unescorted she-male to be seen on the streets of Denver."

The lady in question protested, "Oh, I don't need an escort, Marshal Vail. My own quarters are even closer than our offices and I can transcribe these shorthand notes just as well at home."

Vail shrugged. "You can transcribe 'em on the moon for all I care, as long as I wind up with typewriter English I can show the prosecutor's office in the cold gray dawn, Miss Wiggins. Longarm will see you home anyway."

They'd swung the far end of the cellblock into better light by now and, even if they hadn't, Longarm was more sensitive to she-male feelings than his older, long-married boss. "I suspicion this little lady would just as soon go home on her own, Billy," he said. "I can hail her a hansom cab outside and—"

"You'll take her home," Vail cut in. "And you'll see she's safe behind a locked door with them notes before you leave. Then you'll hunt down one of your drinking companions pounding her beat for the Denver police and make sure the copper badges keep an eye on her aforementioned locked door until I send a deputy for her in the morning. Thanks to you, we have Hard . . . ah, Harrison in the ground and O'Hanlon fixing to do the rope dance. But they wasn't riding *alone* against the Union Pacific, and I'll be mighty chagrined should anything happen to this young lady and her notebook before O'Hanlon's trial."

The girl gasped, "Good heavens!"

Longarm took her gently by one elbow. She didn't look like a fainter, but the floor was cement and he couldn't help noticing her waistline was corseted beyond reason for such an informal occasion. "Billy's just an old mother hen, Miss Wiggins," he said. "But he's right about not taking needless chances. So I'll just carry you home, lock you in, and we'll say no more about it, hear?"

She didn't answer. Now that she could see the awful thing better she found it hard to believe a man so clean-cut and, well, good-looking, could talk so dirty. Longarm looked more like a cowhand dressed for the city than a federal employee, wearing a tobacco tweed suit over his stovepipe boots and cross-draw gun rig. But his rugged suntanned face was clean and smooth-shaven, save for a rather imposing moustache. Miss Wiggins had never crossed the big deputy, so she was unaware how gun-muzzle cold those wide-set innocent gray eyes could stare at less attractive people. Had they met at a Sunday meeting on the green she'd have been pleased indeed to shake with him. But for such a high-toned-looking gent, he sure could talk disgusting!

The three of them left the house of detention and Billy Vail waited politely until Longarm had waved down an open carriage and helped the stenographer in. Miss Wiggins shot Longarm a surprised look when he gave the cab driver her home address. As they drove off up the moonlit street, she asked him how he knew where she lived. He smiled gently down at her and said, "Had to check you out before we picked you in particular to take down O'Hanlon's self-incrimination, Miss Wiggins. Aside from being the slickest shorthand taker in the pool, you're known to keep to your own self. We didn't want a gal given to idle gossip or even a gal with a roommate, if it could be avoided. I don't have to tell you, even a court-appointed lawyer is going to dig some, to see if he can bust the not-too-ironbound case we have against that little skunk, as it is."

She grimaced. "I hope I don't have to appear in court against him. It's bad enough having to transcribe the dirty talk I had to take down. I'd never be able to repeat it in front of a judge and jury!"

He chuckled. "You'll just have to sign a deposition saying you're a qualified court stenographer and that you took down what was said at the time and place indicated. You won't be called as a witness. Neither side will want you to be. As to the dirty parts, you won't have to transcribe the whole tedious conversation. The court will only be interested in the last few minutes of conversation, where O'Hanlon tells us he rode with Harrison in that north pass job and then proves it by saying where his leader went, with what, after. The law calls that guilty knowledge. You can't just *suspicion* a gent for taking part in a train robbery, and witnesses have been known to be wrong. But when a man allows to knowing things only a guilty party could know, he sort of puts his head in the noose for you, see?"

She shuddered. "Brrr! Did I do all that with my own little pencil stub? I don't recall him saying anything about killing anyone. The two of you mostly talked about more disgusting notions."

He said, "I know. I was blushing inside, myself, knowing a lady was listening next door. O'Hanlon didn't have

18

to confess to murder. That was automatic, once he allowed he'd taken part in the robbery. A U. S. postal clerk got gunned in the mail car and the law says it don't matter who actually pulled the trigger. As to why I had to talk so disgusting, that was razzle-dazzle. Folks hardly ever confess anything to a cellmate they take for a Methodist minister."

Before she could answer, they'd pulled up in front of her nearby rooming house. Longarm paid the driver for the short ride and helped her down to the sandstone walk. As the carriage drove off, she stood there awkwardly, staring up at him in the moonlight. "We should have walked. There's so much I didn't get to ask, and . . ."

"Ask away," he replied. "I ain't going anywhere important, Miss Wiggins. Why don't we just set on your front steps a spell whilst I try to satisfy your she-male curiosity?"

"Good heavens, at this hour? I'd cause less of a scandal if I invited you in!"

"Well, you can figure most of it out as you transcribe your shorthand, most likely. Just remember, the early and dirtier parts don't have to appear in the court records. The idle conversation up to the time old Billy showed up as my counselor was just to set the punk up. Make sure you don't have me actually calling my visitor a *lawyer*. Any old pal can *counsel* a boy locked up by mistake, and we're walking a mighty thin legal line as it is."

She sighed and said, "Oh, dear, you'd best come up a spell. I'm never going to get it on paper right until I get it right in my head!"

So they went on up to her second story flat. As she struck a match to light the gas lamp by her door, Longarm saw that her modest private digs were tastefully if inexpensively furnished. Living alone, she only had one main room with an adjoining bath and tiny kitchen. She told him to sit down and go ahead and smoke while she dropped her notes on a table and went into the kitchen to put the coffee on. He didn't think she meant for him to sit on the brass bedstead that was taking up a quarter of the room, so he sat on the sofa near the window instead. He naturally tossed his Stetson aside, but didn't unbuckle his gun rig, lest she get the notion he was getting notions.

He'd just lit a three-for-a-nickel cheroot when she came back in, sat down beside him, and said, "We'll have coffee and cake in a minute. I thought you told that outlaw you were leaving him all your tobacco, Longarm."

He said, "I lied, and my friends call me Custis, Miss . . . ah . . . ?"

"Oh, dear, I was hoping you wouldn't ask. My parents named me Penelope. Don't ask me why."

"I'll call you Penny. Even Penelope beats Custis as a sensible name. The Indians do it less painfully. Indian mamas call their kids anything handy till they're full-grown. Then the kids get to pick their own grown-up names. Some of 'em are sort of silly, but at least it's their own notion."

She dimpled and said, "I didn't know that. It makes a lot of sense, though. I certainly could have come up with something nicer than Penelope Wiggins had it been left to me. But let's get back to business. You said something about what we did tonight being illegal?"

"Not illegal, Miss Penny, just sort of close to unconstitutional. I don't want to go over all the naughty things I might have said in that cell with a lady. Not with the lamp lit, leastways. But as you transcribe it privately, later, I want the fact established that I never—repeat, *never*—admitted to a federal crime. I said right out that I was in that cell due to a misunderstanding, that I wasn't likely to appear before any federal or local court of law, and that I was getting out without even posting a bond because I shouldn't have been in there in the first place."

She brightened. "Oh, I see! If you'd said you were, say, a bank robber, his lawyers could accuse us of entrapment, right?"

He nodded. "The blotter will show I came in willingly to clear up a possible misunderstanding about my love life and that as soon as Marshal Vail was notified he told 'em to turn me loose, as the federal government had no charge worth mention against me. There's another sort of interesting technicality as allows you to just forget my name when you types up the testimony you just happened to overhear as you were knitting or something within earshot. When a U. S. citizen is arrested on a false charge and released for lack of evidence, it's lawful as well as common courtesy to expunge his identity from the files. So you just heard Stretch O'Hanlon bragging about his wicked past with a temporary visitor and likely harmless vagrant called Shorty."

"Who bragged about his own wicked past in a wicked way indeed." She nodded primly, but with a certain twinkle in her eye.

He said, "I told you that was razzle-dazzle. I had to be in that cell with him for *some* infernal reason, and I just explained why I couldn't confess to any *real* federal offense. I counted on him being noble-natured enough to assume such a downright dirty rascal as he found himself locked in with had to be in as much trouble as him. We knew O'Hanlon, like lots of self-appointed Robin Hoods, considered himself a gent when it came to women and children. He got them nicks in his gun grips shooting *men* in the back a lot, but he was so shocked by my unseemly talk it threw him off guard."

"It shocked me, too. And I almost dropped my pencil when *you* were the one who kept bringing up police informants!"

21

Longarm chuckled and said, "That was what stage magicians call misdirection or what writers call taking it out of the reader's head in advance. Have you ever started a book where it says, 'You ain't never going to believe this, it sounds like such a whopper,' just as you're about to toss the book aside as a plain impossible yarn?"

She laughed. "I'm surprised to hear you read books, Custis. Somehow, you don't seem the type. You still haven't explained why you had to . . . well, lay on the dirty parts so much. I mean, sure, saying you were there on a trumped-up morals charge makes sense. But that business about the vile manners of the federal convicts was—"

"To shake him up so he wasn't thinking straight," Longarm cut in. "O'Hanlon's not a total idjet when he's thinking calm. But he's little, sort of girlish-looking, and helpless as a kitten without his guns. So we figured he'd be worried about what might happen to his honor once he got to Leavenworth. It was Marshal Vail's idea to lock him in with a bigger, tougher-looking man, and scare him even more. In the end, as you noted, he was so anxious to stay on the good side of me, and beg me to get him out when he saw, or thought that he saw I had pull, that the poor little rascal forgot all about who he might or might not be talking to, about what."

He saw the room was murking up with his tobacco smoke, the windows being closed and the drapes drawn, so he stubbed out his cheroot as he added, "Had we given him a minute to think with his limited brain instead of his twitching nerves, he might have figured out there was no way on earth we could hold him for more than seventy-two hours on suspicion and, until he confessed to guilty knowledge, that's all we *had* on the rascal. I'm sorry we had to put your delicate ears through so much unseemly dictation. But if it's any comfort to them now, Stretch O'Hanlon will never get the chance to kill anybody, male or she-male, again."

She nodded soberly. "Maybe it's just as well. I know the boy's a killer, but I can't help feeling a little sorry for him. He was so weak, and so frightened, Custis."

Longarm shrugged. "That railroad postal clerk likely felt weak and scared, too, when they gunned him down like a dog. But look on the brighter side, Miss Penny. You heard O'Hanlon say how scared he was about going to prison. Thanks to your help, he don't have to worry about that no more. The hangman will make sure he meets his maker with his manly honor intact."

She grimaced. "My God, you do enjoy disgusting conversation, don't you? I think the coffee should be ready now."

Chapter 3

Longarm gazed after her fondly as she rose to fetch the refreshments. He didn't see why, since he'd told her the answers to all her questions. At least he thought he had, until she returned with the coffee and cake on a tray, placed them on a little sissy rosewood table by the sofa, and for no reason Longarm could fathom, said, "You may as well know that I heard all about you and that blonde in the Land Management Office, Custis."

He frowned thoughtfully and silently as he watched her pour. She handed him his cup and added, "Well?"

"This is mighty fine coffee, ma'am," he said. "Arbuckle or some other fancy Frisco brand, right?"

"It's Arbuckle. Do you deny you had an affair with that other stenographer down the hall from your own office?"

He picked up a slice of coffee cake, bit it and washed it down. "I never deny nor confirm gossip about a lady, ma'am," he said. "No matter what I say, I might be making a liar out of them. So I'll tell you what. You just ask that other gal what she recalls about working in the same building with us and, whatever she says happened, I'll swear to it."

Penny laughed despite herself. "That's another thing I heard about you. They say nobody can get you to say for sure which side you even rode for in the War."

He shrugged. "Well, it was over fifteen years ago, and old war stories tend to be old bore stories, Miss Penny. As for men who boast of their less dangerous adventures with unarmed she-male civilians, I consider a kiss-and-tell gent lower than a sidewinder's vest pockets."

"In other words, it's nobody's business what's been going on between you and that blonde in the Land Office?"

He washed down another bite of cake before he replied. "If anything was, it'd be her business and mine. But, at the risk of sounding like a big old blabbermouth, you can tell the other gals in the pool that, as of the moment, nothing's going on between me and any gal working in the federal building." Which was the simple truth, when he thought about it. For not one of the three gals he'd been sleeping with regular were working in the federal building at this hour.

He wasn't sure whether he wanted to try for four, even if this one kept sending smoke signals against the blue-sky innocence of those big old eyes staring at him. He polished off the cake and washed it down to say, "Well, that surely hit the spot, Miss Penny. I'd best go see if I can find a sober beat copper to keep an eye on your door once I leave."

She said, "It's early. Would you answer me truthfully if I asked you a sort of . . . well . . . intimate question no names need be attached to?"

He shrugged. "I can try. I hardly know any dirty stories about folks I don't know, though."

She said soberly, "I think you do. Do you know why you shocked me so, back there at the house of detention, Custis?"

"Sure. I was talking dirty. I told you why. How many times do you expect me to say I'm sorry?"

"I'm a grown woman, Custis. *We* tell dirty stories, too," she said. "I'll confess I just chuckled at some of the things you said, until you got to that part about the young girl."

He smiled sheepishly. "Thunderation, I just made that up out of thin air, Miss Penny! Did you really think I was the sort of gent who'd trifle with children, for God's sake?"

25

She shook her head, but said, "I could tell you were making up a tall tale. But some of what you said, alas, was all too true and it . . . well, hit close to home."

Then she reached up to unpin her hair and let it fall down in raven's wings to her waist, framing her cameo features in a silky cathedral arch of ebony waves.

There were smoke signals and there were open invitations, in a world where women didn't let down their hair until they were fixing to go to bed. So Longarm just reeled her in, kissed her full on her warm, willing lips, and, when they came up for air, murmured, "I don't recall entirely what I made up about that imaginary little gal. But I sure must have said something smart as hell."

She snuggled closer as she murmured sort of sadly, "Whether you ever broke in a girl that young or not, you certainly gave away a lot you know about women. You can see I'm naturally shy and . . . oh, Custis, I've been so lonely since I had to leave my old home town. You see, once I'd tasted the pleasures of love, I couldn't stop. It was just as you said. Once a boy or girl learns why boys and girls are different, they can't ever go back to childhood again, and . . . Where are you taking me, Custis?"

That seemed like a mighty dumb question, since the bedstead was just a few feet away. But, as he carried her over to it, he soothed, "Nowhere you don't want to go, Miss Penny."

Then he lowered her to the mattress, kissed her again to make sure they were still friends, and rose to move to the gas lamp to trim it. As he plunged the room into darkness Penny gasped, "My God, don't you even want to hear how I went wrong, back home?"

He rejoined her on the bed, shucking some of his duds before he ever got there, and, as he discovered she was still half dressed, proceeded to help her out of her unmention-

26

ables as he said, "You ain't back home now, honey. So let's not rake up our misspent childhoods. No offense, but the tale gets sort of tedious once you've heard it a time or more. I wish I knew why you gals wear these infernal whalebone corsets and how in thunder a man's supposed to get 'em off you in the dark. But such details can wait, I reckon, you sweet little thing."

As he kicked off the last of his own underwear and rolled in place between her trembling but widespread silk-sheathed thighs, Penny said, "It was a minister's son who led me down the primrose path. I swore I'd never do it again. But it felt so good, even though he'd acted ugly, and..."

"Them minister's sons will do it every time." Longarm mounted her, adding. "But let's not bring no other folk to bed with us just now, honey. For I want you all to myself, and... Jesus, are you sure you ain't a virgin?"

"Oh, you're hurting me! You're too big! I mean, all over, and... Stop it! I can't take it! You're hurting me! It feels like you're splitting me wide open, and, oh Jesus, I *love* it!"

He'd figured she might like it better once it was all the way in. But he posted gentle in the saddle at first, since it was obvious she hadn't had as much practice as him, lately. Penny started moving her own hips in a manner that assured him that, like roller skating, once a body had done it good, the skill was never lost entire.

She climaxed almost at once, sobbed thankfully, and begged for more. So he did his best to oblige and knew he was obliging her right when she came ahead of him again and then with him. As he lay soaking in her trembling charms he decided this was as good a time as any to finish shucking her totally.

Having stripped her entirely, he hooked an elbow under each of Penny's knees to spread them wide. She gasped,

27

"This is impossible! No normal woman could take it this deep and live! But for some reason it doesn't even hurt, and ... Yes ... Yes ... Harder, deeper!"

He did his best, but when they finally recovered their sanity and lay side by side across the rumpled sheets she nuzzled her face deeper into the fold of his bare shoulder. She sighed and murmured, "You must think I'm low as any whore you've ever been with, now. I don't know how I'll ever be able to face you at work after throwing myself at you so shamelessly."

He patted her bare rump fondly. "Well, for openers, you can just say 'Howdy.' I told you I don't gossip about my friends."

"How many other friends have you done this to, you brute?"

"If I told you that would be gossiping. Let's lay some ground rules while we're breathing regular, Miss Penny. If you don't ever want to do this with me again, just say so and I'll understand. Lots of notions we get late at night don't seem so great the next morning."

"What if I said I wanted you to come back tomorrow night?"

"I'd surely have to, for I don't have anything better planned."

She stiffened. "You bastard! Are you saying you still mean to do this with other girls on other nights?"

"Now just simmer down. If I do have other nights like this with someone else, you'll never hear of it. Just like they'll never hear of you and me tonight. Don't try to pin me down to anything more definite, honey."

She sniffed and said, "I might have known you were just using me. You men are all alike once you've had your way with a woman."

He grimaced up at the dark ceiling. "Yeah, I've noticed

coming is confined exclusive to just one sex. I'm sure sorry I abused you, ma'am. Now if only I can recall where in hell I left my pants, I'll just get out of your way so's you can get to work on that shorthand Marshal Vail is expecting, transcribed, in about six or seven hours."

She gasped. "My God, I'd forgotten all about that! I'm going to be up half the night now. But . . . could we try it one more time before you have to leave, darling?"

He did. So it was well after two A.M. when they parted in her doorway and he went down into the brighter moonlight to scout up a copper. He doubted anyone could be gunning for such a sweet little thing, but he had his orders. On the outside chance any sidekicks of the late Hard-Ass Henry Harrison were in town, he sure didn't want them gunning anybody *he* wasn't mad at.

He circled the block twice before he spotted a blue-uniformed member of the Denver force strolling his way, strumming a picket fence with his billy. They knew each other, so the beat man said he'd be proud to keep an eye on Miss Wiggin's door. They shook on it and Longarm headed south toward the less fashionable part of town where he hired his own furnished digs.

But he'd only strode a block and half along the dark, deserted street when a black cat brought him good luck. The black cat didn't cross his path. It lay dead on the walk ahead of him, smelling awful despite the cool night air. Longarm didn't care why it was dead. Killing cats was hardly a federal offense. But he swung wide to avoid it, so the bullet meant for his back snarled past him by a close but comfortable margin.

Longarm didn't look back toward the pistol report he'd just heard behind him. He reversed direction to dive into the black shadows of a deep storefront opening just as the mysterious pistol went off again without, as far as Longarm

29

could tell, hitting anything important to him.

As he got his new bearings, Longarm could see that he was boxed. The other gunslick knew where he was, but Longarm lacked the same advantage. Sticking his head out right now could be injurious to his health.

He drew his own double-action .44-40 anyway and risked a discreet peek around the edge of the storefront. He ducked back fast as a pistol flash down the street and the spang of hot lead on timber told him the other son of a bitch had mighty fine night vision. There had to be a better way.

Longarm fished in his pocket with his free hand and took out a jackknife the law would have arrested most folk for packing. He unfolded the blade filed to a skeleton key and tried the lock of the door he was pinned against. It worked. Longarm let himself into the deserted store, shut and re-locked the door, then headed back through the racks of what looked like women's notions to see if there was a back door.

There was. It led, as he'd hoped, to a back alley. He moved down the alley, crunching cinders as, somewhere in the night, a tinny police whistle started howling at the moon.

Longarm didn't want the Denver police blundering into a gunfight blind. He knew where his enemy was, now. But rounding a corner on a business street shuttered and unin-habited for the night could take fifty years off the average policeman's life.

Longarm counted back doors until he had the right num-ber, then let himself into the back of a tailor ship. He hoped the tailor didn't live over the shop as he fumbled his way forward through dark unfamiliar surroundings, making as much noise as an unskilled burglar. But nobody yelled at him and within a few moments he'd worked his way to the front door. Better yet, it was a glass door, so he had an interesting view of the gent, who was dressed cow, crouch-ing in yet another doorway on the far side of the deserted thoroughfare.

Longarm didn't even have to pick the front door of the tailor shop. It opened silently from inside. So he just stepped out, gun leveled on the man across the way, and called out, "Freeze!"

It didn't work. The man across the street jumped like a spooked colt and came down waving his own gun about, hunting desperately for the source of Longarm's voice. Longarm snorted in disgust and shot him.

The tall deputy had aimed low, hoping to enjoy a serious conversation with the son of a bitch as they waited for the ambulance wagon. But he could tell from the way the other fell, limp as a wet rag doll, that his round had carried a mite high.

He strolled across to the man on the stone walk, keeping his own gun trained on the rascal anyway. He heard running footsteps and a voice calling out, "Down this way, Bradford!"

Longarm called back, "Hold your fire, Denver! It's over and I'm law, too!"

Then he knelt, felt the side of the dead man's throat, and holstered his own gun. He could reload later. Some copper badges could make grim mistakes when they met up with drawn guns in the gloom.

He'd just rolled the body on its back and patted it down for identification when two of Denver's finest joined them. Fortunately, they both knew Longarm of old, which saved lots of tedious explanations. But they still wanted to know who he'd shot and why. Longarm said, "Don't know for sure, boys. His wallet says he's named Jones, but he don't look like a Jones to me."

The senior Denver peace officer hunkered down for a better look before he opined, "He's dressed cow. But them's fancy boots and a mighty fancy vest for an honest cowhand to be wearing. That new Stetson's creased Montana style. You made any recent enemies up Montana way, Longarm?"

Longarm took out his gun again to reload the spent chamber as he replied laconically, "I make friends all over, packing a badge for Uncle Sam. His face is unfamiliar to me, though. I'm sure I'd remember anyone so ugly had I ever seen him in the flesh or aboard a wanted poster."

"Well, whoever he was, he must have been gunning for you personal, Longarm," the other copper said.

Longarm chuckled. "Do tell? I thought he might have mistaken me for a *duck* just now. I don't reckon you boys could see fit to sort of take charge here and let me go on home to bed?"

The two Denver lawmen just stared at him, so he sighed and said, "All right, let's get the son of a bitch down to the morgue so's I can make a statement for your damned old coroner before it's time to go to work some more!"

One of the coppers chuckled sympathetically and observed, "You do look a mite weary, Longarm. I take it you've had a hard night?"

Longarm shrugged. "It was hard enough a few minutes ago. Right now I'm just plain tired."

Chapter 4

Longarm didn't get to bed alone until nearly four in the morning. So, though he tried his best not to, he overslept a mite and wound up reporting for work about noon the next day. The prissy clerk who played the typewriter out front had already gone to lunch, so Longarm was spared his usual "now-you're-gonna-get-it!" look as he strode boldly into the back office to take his usual chewing like a man.

Billy Vail glanced up from behind his cluttered desk, didn't even look at the banjo clock on the wall, and said, "I heard. I'm impressed. How in thunder do you drill a man direct through the heart at that range in the dark?"

Longarm said, "Easy. You aim for the balls. Any line on who he used to be yet?"

Vail shook his head. "We seem to be suffering a plague of Smiths and Joneses of late," he said wryly. "Police photographer sent us a picture of his no doubt unusually peaceable expression for our files, but I haven't been able to line his ugly mug up with anyone Uncle Sam is interested in. What were you doing in that part of town at that hour, by the way?"

"Just strolling, Billy. Any law against a moonlight stroll on the Denver statutes?"

"Don't shit me, boy. The Denver Directory puts Miss Penelope Wiggins's home address less than three blocks from where you was window shopping or whatever when you met up with the late Mr. Jones. Fortunately for you, the gal showed up a lot earlier than you this morning, with them shorthand notes transcribed neat as hell, considering how puffy-eyed she was. I told you plain out just to take her, damn it, home!"

"Hell, Billy, that's the only place I took her. Why are you staring at me so suspicious?"

Vail snorted and replied, "Suspicious, hell. I know damn well what you done, you horny rascal. But that's neither here nor there. I hope the two of you got enough office romancing out of your systems for now. For I'm sending you up north on a field case that ought to keep at least the *gal* out of trouble for a spell."

Longarm sat in the leather guest chair near Vail's desk and fished out a smoke. "I sure wish you wouldn't do that, Billy. I thought we'd agreed Sheriff Lansford up in Middle Fork could wrap up the loose ends on that railroad job for us."

Vail rummaged for a yellow Western Union form, waved it, and said, "He's already done so, whilst you was slug-a-bed half a working day. It was no chore for a savvy old lawman to find out the name of Harrison's only gal in town, once he was told to look it up. Lansford and his men paid an early visit on the whore and she was so anxious to stay out of jail during her busy season she cooperated in full. Middle Fork's recovered all the loot we'll ever recover, now. Harrison had hid it under a floorboard, like we suspected."

Longarm nodded and said, "I never suspected he was long on brains after that time he slapped leather on me while I had the drop on him. But if you don't want me to go up to the Dakotas about the South Pass train robbery, what *do* you want me to do up there?"

"I ain't sending you to the Dakota Territory. I'm sending you up to Montana this time. You recall that Wendigo case you solved for the B.I.A. a spell back?"

Longarm frowned. "I do, and I solved it too good to have to solve it again. The so-called Wendigo pestering them Blackfoot was a white man, not a devil like they thought, and I killed him permanent. So that can't be why you want me to go up there again, right?"

Vail nodded. "The B.I.A. has no complaints about the way you ended the spooky career of the so-called Wendigo and the other white crooks working with him to steal Indian land, Longarm. What the Indian agent up that way is bitching about now is other Indians. Plains Cree, from Canada. They've been encroaching on the hunting grounds of our own sweet Blackfeet and, unless something's done about it pronto, we're facing a full-scale Indian war on our north border. I don't have to tell you how, once one tribe gets to shooting at another, any *whites* in the way tend to wind up deader, faster. Neither Plains Cree nor Blackfoot can be said to admire white civilization all that much. Both tribes have been tamed recent and, in their Shining Times, both were unusually truculent, even for Horse Indians. They are evenly matched when it comes to being able to kill one another. A white nester or even a cowhand meeting a Blackfoot or Plains Cree on the warpath would be meat on the table many a surly young brave would find hard to pass up. So the B.I.A. wants the mess nipped in the bud, and you're the nipper they picked."

Longarm lit his cheroot, shook out the match, and said, "Billy, you're talking silly . . . no offense. I'm good, but I ain't that good. Taking on two truculent tribes at once is a job for the cavalry, not this poor lonesome cowboy."

"You ain't a cowboy," Vail replied. "You're a deputy U. S. marshal and the situation up there along the border is too delicate for the yellow legs. The army can't round up the Blackfoot and herd 'em back on their reserve because they're already *on* their damned reserve. And this time both

35

the B.I.A. and the War Department agree *our* Indians are in the *right!*"

Longarm blew a thoughtful smoke ring. "That sounds fair. So why can't the cavalry go after the *Cree* and chase 'em back to Canada? Come to think on it, why in thunder would Canadian Indians want to ride south of their border in the first damn place? Far be it from me to criticize the Bureau of Indian Affairs, but Canada's always treated its own Indians better."

The older, fatter Vail chewed his older, fatter unlit stogie as he chose his words delicately. "Them was the good old days. The current conservative Macdonald administration up Canada way has new Indian policy, a budding civil war on its hands, and a Pacific Railway to finish. So the Cree feel unwanted and they want to live down here. But the new hunting grounds they've picked just happen to be the northwest corner of Montana that the Great White Father said the Blackfoot could have as long as the grass growed, the rivers ran, or at least as long as they behaved their fool selves."

Longarm shrugged and said, "You're talking in circles, boss. I ain't interested in the motives of Canadian Indians. They don't come under our jurisdiction and you just said the Blackfoot, who do, are behaving themselves. If the U. S. has been invaded by Indians or Eskimos it's a job for the War Department, not Justice. So I ain't going."

Vail said, "Yes, you are. A while back you avenged the murder of the Blackfoot chief, Real Bear, and saved the whole tribe from a land grab disguised as bad medicine that had 'em nervous as hell. So you're one of the few white men who can still sit in council with their tribal leaders and hope to emerge with all his hair in place."

Longarm shook his head and said, "That well may be, as far as the Blackfoot enter into the debate. But what pull could I possibly have with the invading *Cree?* It's a fool's errand, Billy. You could send a Blackfoot medicine man in the flesh up there to shake his prayer sticks at 'em, and they'd still put on their paint! Hell's bells, the Hopi are so peaceable it's what their name *means* in Pueblo. But no white man born of mortal woman could stop even the Hopi from fighting if their lands were being invaded. The Apache found that out a long time ago."

"Don't change the subject. The B.I.A. didn't request your services in calming the Hopi this time. They want you to keep your Blackfoot pals calmed down until Washington can work out a peaceful solution with Canada."

Longarm snorted in disgust. "That'll be the day! Old Macdonald got his fool self elected in Canada on anti-American slogans. The time you sent me up there to arrest a killer I almost got arrested by the Mounties. If I was President Hayes I'd just send the cavalry up there with orders to chase them Cree back where they belong."

Vail said, "You ain't President Hayes. You don't even run this office." He sighed and added, "Sometimes it don't feel like *I* do, either. I don't disagree with you totally, old son, but it's out of my hands. The B.I.A. asked for you. Washington told me to send you. So, when Henry comes back from lunch, he'll be typing up your travel orders."

Longarm grimaced and said, "Knowing Henry, he's likely already typed 'em. He works overtime to get me out of the office, the sissy rascal. But I still ain't going. There's nothing sensible I can do up there, and last night some son of a bitch tried to gun me *here!* You're all too right about it taking place too close for comfort to Miss Penelope Wiggins's doorstep. That means the rascal had her place staked out. That means I ain't about to leave town before I find out why."

"Oh, hell, Longarm, people are always shooting you in

the back," his boss said. "That last unfortunate rascal *couldn't* have been waiting for you outside that stenographer's door, when you study on it. If he had been, he'd have tried to gun you as you came out buttoning up your pants, not nearly three blocks away, right?"

Longarm nodded grudgingly, but said, "Just the same, it was too close for comfort. I'd best stick around until after the grand jury's read her transcribed notes and deposition, at least. By then nobody will have a sensible reason for gunning the little gal, see?"

Vail shook his head. "I see you ain't had her in every odd position yet, you bullshitting lothario! The late Mr. Jones had no known connection with young O'Hanlon or the late Hard-Ass Henry's gang. He was after you for other reasons of his own you'd have been able to ask him about if you didn't shoot at folks so serious."

Longarm blew smoke out of his nostrils like an annoyed bull and insisted, "Saying he had no known connection with the case Penny's working on ain't good enough. We don't even know what his right name might have been. So, like I said, I ain't leaving town just yet. And, like the Indians say, I have spoken."

Vail scowled and roared, "You'll go where I *order* you to go, you mule-headed son of a bitch! Who in thunder do you think you are to tell your senior officer where you choose to go or not go?"

Longarm shrugged. "An ex-federal employee, I reckon. You can take my badge and shove it. But me and my guns are staying here in Denver till I know for sure I haven't got a pretty little gal killed."

"Jesus Christ, Longarm, does Penny Wiggins mean *that* much to you?"

"She means no more nor less than other ladies I know or, for that matter, the beat copper I asked to keep an eye on her. No man has the right to get another human being in a dangerous fix and then run off to Montana on 'em."

"Longarm, there ain't a shred of evidence that anyone's after anyone but you!"

"There ain't a shred of evidence that folks I drag into my affairs is *safe*, neither. I ain't leaving town till I know for sure. I mean it."

Longarm rose to his considerable height, took out his wallet, and unpinned his federal badge to drop it on Vail's desk, saying, "I'm going out to ask questions along Larimer Street now, Billy. That man I gunned last night was afoot in riding duds. So he must have left at least one mount in one livery stable, and there's no telling what a High Plains drifter might or might not have in his saddlebags. You do what you want with that badge. I ain't working for you till I tidy up my personal life a mite."

He turned and strode out as behind him Vail roared, "Come back here, you asshole! Desertion ain't allowed in this department!"

Longarm paid him no mind. One of the things he'd disliked most about army life had been the way they could shoot an old boy who left to take care of more important business. Working for the Justice Department had been all right. But, what the hell, he was still young enough to hire on as a top hand once he settled things here in town. Herding cows didn't pay quite as well. But, on the other hand, hardly any cows ever tried to shoot a man in the back.

Outside the federal building the noonday sun was trying to fry eggs on the granite steps. Longarm paused in the doorway, blinking to let his eyes adjust to the glare. It was a habit he'd picked up without having to study why, once he'd come west after the War. The contrast between indoors and out was considerable on a clear cloudless summer day a mile above sea level. So it could pay to get one's eyes

39

working right before one barged out a doorway into the bright unknown.

This time it paid well indeed. For as Longarm stood there blinking and rolling his eyes up at the dazzling skyline across the street in hopes of seeing the slightly shadier street itself a lot better, he noticed a blur of motion atop one of the flat rooftops over there. He'd hardly ever noticed a chimney or air vent moving enough to matter, at high noon or any other time. So he moved back inside quickly and made for the nearest stairwell. He went up the marble stairs three at a time, to the surprise of some office gals coming down. But when one of them called a question after him he didn't stop to answer, even though she'd been sort of pretty.

The fancy federal marble ended in practical steel steps once he'd risen higher than the general public was allowed to go. As he'd remembered, the black tin door leading out to the flat roof of the federal building opened to the east, away from the prevailing west winds as well as out of the line of sight from the rooftop he was more concerned about at the moment. This one was hot as the hinges of hell. Longarm crawled across it on his hands and knees to keep his rump below the level of the parapet provided by a federal architect who couldn't have known what he was doing when he designed this particular building. The roofing was supposed to be white gravel. The sun had boiled the tar mixed in with it sticky. Longarm crawled to the parapet, rubbed his hands on his tweed-covered thighs as he knelt there, then drew his .44-40 and took off his Stetson.

The Colorado sun slammed down to fry his dark wavy hair as Longarm gingerly had a look-see over the stone parapet. The view was interesting as hell. The federal building was a full story higher than the brick rooming house across the way. So the son of a bitch over there with a buffalo gun still trained on the entrance below wasn't even

40

looking up as Longarm aimed the .44-40 both hands, wrists braced on solid granite, and called out loudly, "You on that roof! Let go that rifle and grab some sky as you stand up, still as hell!"

The startled bushwhacker across the gulf between them looked up, saw who was speaking to him, and made a dumb move with his buffalo gun. So Longarm's smaller weapon knocked him away from it and he writhed like a worm caught by sunrise on a sidewalk for a spell until Longarm noticed he was writhing toward the open roof hatch over yonder and called out again, "Hold it right there, pilgrim! I still got four rounds trained on you, and you must have guessed by now I'm a tolerable shot!."

The wounded man sat up, raised one hand in submission as he braced his weight on the other, and called, "Don't shoot! I need a doctor bad!"

Longarm called back, "Not as bad as you will if you move another inch toward that hatch! Just stay put while I figure out how the rest of this works. There ought to be one of them newfangled telephones up here, but there ain't."

Down below, a police whistle was blowing. Longarm grinned and called out, "There you go. It's getting so you can't hardly have a shootout in downtown Denver in private, these days."

Longarm was trying to keep an eye on his distant prisoner and spot a city lawman down below at the same time when he heard gravel crunch behind him and spun, startled, to train his gun on one of the uniformed federal building guards, who froze and blurted, "I heard gunshots from up here, Longarm."

Longarm looked disgusted. "No, you didn't. I only fired once. I'll explain in a minute. I'm busy right now."

Then he turned his attention back where it belonged and groaned, "Stupid son of a bitch! Not you. Me!" He rose to

41

his feet and ran for the stairs.

Behind him, the bewildered guard called out, "What's going on? I don't see nothing going on around here. Hey, ain't that a white sombrero laying on that roof across the way?"

Longarm didn't answer. He dashed down the steps five or six at a time, one hand on the rail and the other waving a sixgun as the few people he met going down got out of his way.

Longarm didn't go out the front entrance. He wasn't as excited as he looked. He went all the way to the basement and dashed out a service entrance to cross the street at a hopefully unexpected run to tear into the rooming house next door rather than the one in question. A colored cleaning woman gasped in dismay as the tall deputy barged past her in the dark hallway, snapping, "Get behind a door and lock it, hear?" before he tore out the back door into the cinder-covered alley, saw nothing but a fresh pile of horseshit steaming near a next-door telegraph pole, and muttered, "Thunderation!"

Longarm tore into the rooming house the gunslick had doubtless just tore out of and, sure enough, a trail of blood spatters led like red ants on the warpath all the way from the back door to the stairs.

A brassy-looking blonde in a kimono a gal that fat should have kept less open down the front met Longarm on the stairs to ask, "Where do you think you're going, cowboy?"

"Your roof," Longarm said. "I ain't a cowboy. I'm the law. Who are you?"

"*You* can call me sweetheart, handsome. But my official name is Mame and, while I'm open to better offers, I'm the landlady here. Do you know who might have been shooting guns around here lately, lover?"

Longarm eased past her to mount the stairs. "Jesus, one

42

bitty shot and the whole infernal neighborhood gets to asking tedious questions," he muttered.

The blonde followed him up, as was her right, he supposed. Since she could only take the steps two at a time, Longarm beat her easily to the roof and was standing there holding a new Stetson and wearing a disgusted expression by the time she'd joined him there to ask again what was going on.

He said, "I just blowed a bushwhacker out from under this expensive hat. There ought to be a rifle around here, too, and . . . There she is, over behind that sewer-gas vent."

He crunched across the tarpaper, holstering his own revolver as he bent to pick up the .50 caliber Express. The blonde must have known something about guns. She whistled softly and observed, "Anyone packing a piece like that was out to do bodily harm to someone else, I'd say."

Longarm said, "Yeah. Me. He had it trained on them bronze doors across the way. And, I ask you, do I look like a *buffalo?*"

She laughed sort of lewdly. "You're better looking, though you ain't much smaller. Are them shoulders real, handsome?"

"My name's Custis, Custis Long, and never mind about my shoulders. How come you never noticed that other gent traipsing up and down your stairs if you noticed me so good, Miss Mame?"

The blonde shrugged, almost spilling a heroic naked breast out the front of her loosely fastened kimono. "I was taking a bath in my private quarters until I heard a gunshot and somebody running like hell outside my door. Just what are you accusing me of, handsome?"

He shook his head and said, "If he'd had your blessings he'd have been staked out in an upstairs window, not on the roof, and we might not be having this conversation. But let's talk about your other boarders. I couldn't help noticing how empty your hallways was downstairs, considering."

Mame nodded. "They'd *better* be at this hour. I don't rent rooms on credit. I rent mostly to working-class transients and, as you might have noticed, this is the middle of a working day, so everyone's out to work. Nobody figures to get home till after five or six. We have the whole place to ourselves, and . . . Say, ain't you the Long they call Longarm across the street? This *is* a pleasure! I've heard a lot about you, Longarm. And now that I see you up close, I find some of it easy to believe. What say we go downstairs and get out of this hot sun and ridiculous vertical position?"

He smiled sheepishly and moved over to the hatchway with her. She had a point, about the sun, at least. The son of a bitch had gotten away, not winged too badly to ride, so there was nothing left to do up here, now.

As he followed the brassy blonde down the stairs, more sedately than he'd climbed them, they both heard someone banging on the front door below. As she went to answer it, Longarm saw, over her plump shoulder, that a couple of coppers and, of all people, Billy Vail were peering in through the glass.

Mame opened the door. Longarm said, "You were right. This was the building. But the rascal got out the back, winged and hatless. If you coppers get cracking, someone may spot him before he can get to cover. Don't know what sort of mount he's riding. But look for a gent dressed cow, new jeans as ain't been laundered more than a few times, light blue hickory shirt and—oh, yeah, bleeding pretty good from a .44-40 slug in his left shoulder."

He handed Vail the rifle and Stetson he'd recovered and added, "These look new, too. He could have bought the Stetson anywhere, but you might be able to trace the serial number of this buffalo gun. They ain't been selling many lately."

44

Vail took charge of the evidence, but said, "Longarm, I sure wish someone would tell me what on earth is going on."

"I'd tell you if I knew," Longarm said. "I'd no sooner left your office to find out who came gunning for me last night than somebody tried to gun me again! Did you ever have the feeling you wasn't popular?"

"It's your own fault for putting so many owlhoots in jail, old son. Let's go back across the street and talk about it some more, huh?"

Longarm shook his head. "Nope. I told you I ain't working for you no more. Leastways, not until I get some answers, my way."

Vail pouted like a mean little kid and said, "All right. The B.I.A. can wait till we find out if this nonsense has anything to do with the O'Hanlon case, I reckon. So come home to papa and all is forgiven, just this once. But if you ever sass me again, you stubborn rascal—"

"We'll talk about it later," Longarm cut in. "You can keep my badge or give it back, as you please. But I'm through jawing. I'm hunting. And I ain't caught half as many killers *in* your office as I have *outside* it, Billy."

Vail called him as vile a name as he could in mixed company, said he'd put some other deputies out to chat with gunsmiths, and grumped off. The local peace officers saw there was nothing much for them to do there, either, so they left, either to look for a wounded saddle tramp or to have some needled beer at the nearby Parthenon, depending on whether one chose to believe them or not.

Mame closed and locked the door, asking, "Are you as masterful with women as you are with men, handsome?"

He said, "Depends on the company I happen to be keeping, Miss Mame."

She turned, wrapped her plump arm around him, and let the kimono open all it cared to as she looked up at him

45

adoringly. "You can keep me company to my quarters then. For I can see it's useless to resist such a natural leader, but I don't want to be caught making love in the durned old hallway!"

He hugged her back to be polite, but in truth he hadn't been planning to make love to the brassy blonde anywhere until he reconsidered his current options.

Longarm wasn't given to false modesty. He'd never seen all that much to admire when he was shaving in the mirror, but who was he to argue with all the ladies who'd said he was good-looking? On the other hand, this brassy blonde was a tolerable looker, too, if a man fancied his she-males well-upholstered enough for the *Police Gazette*. So he couldn't help wondering, despite what other gals had told him, why she was coming on so strong. It hardly seemed possible a decent-looking gal who acted about as shy as a Dodge City dove on payday could be starved for slap and tickle. She'd just said her boarders were mostly day laborers, and she had an established habit of wandering around her all-male rooming house in an open kimono, for God's sake.

So, for the sake of his growing suspicions, Longarm kissed the brassy blonde full on her lush lips, returned her compliments with his own tongue, and allowed he had no place better to go right now.

She led him into the gaudy temptation of her loudly decorated private quarters on the second floor as he made a mental note that it fit her story and where she'd been on the stairs when they'd first met. She told him to make himself at home and, without further ceremony, peeled off her kimono to spread herself for inspection across the counterpane of her big gilt four-poster. The quilted bed cover was fire-engine-red satin. She was blonde all over. Longarm saw he was just going to have to be a sport as more than his suspicions commenced to grow inside his pants. So he took his pants and everything else off.

As he did so, Mame blinked in surprise at his muscular naked body and asked, "Ooh! Is that all for me?"

He laughed, said it sure was, and climbed aboard her with no further ado. For, though he'd risen to the occasion, as any healthy man would have, in truth he didn't have his heart in it this afternoon, even though she praised what he did have in her as he tucked the derringer he'd been holding, palmed, in the crack between the bedboard and the now bouncing mattress. He'd already noticed that the door was locked with a stout-looking barrel bolt. Once he had the added insurance of a sneaky gun of his own handy, he was able to examine the possible witness with less undivided enthusiasm. Whatever she was up to, old Mame sure moved her plump hips up and down mighty fine.

She gasped in mingled pleasure and discomfort as he hooked a muscular forearm under one overly dimpled knee and hauled it higher than it really wanted to go. She said, "Jesus, I think you just dislocated my hip. But my, that does feel nice, the way you're hitting bottom now."

He knew the brassy blonde would have felt even better had he not just had some mighty fine loving less than ten hours earlier, so he tried to treat Mame right.

Mame climaxed awesomely under him, rolling her blonde head from side to side across the red satin as she crooned love words he knew better than to hold her to and then, when she saw he was still going at her hammer and tongs, she gasped, "Oh, Jesus, you're too much for any one woman to handle! It's no wonder all the girls in the federal building across the street speak your name in whispers!"

He let that go, though it cooled him as he considered her words. It stood to reason a lady running a rooming house across the street from the federal building might know some of the folk working there. It was even possible that hearing

47

gossip about him had aroused her horny curiosity. So, yeah, he could be pumping a suspect who only wanted *this* kind of pumping. He'd find out soon enough. Anyone set up to literally catch him with his pants down would be waiting for the bed springs to stop strumming so he could nail the man on the bed without hitting the woman.

As he rolled off Mame, derringer once more palmed down at his side away from her heaving form, he said, "I got to get my second wind, little darling. You're too much woman for one man to handle, too."

She stretched and yawned like a fat contented cat and said innocently enough, "I think we might be establishing a legend. Jesus, you're good. If I didn't know better, I'd be willing to swear you hadn't had a woman in at least a month!"

He managed to keep obvious suspicion from his voice as he replied in a desperately casual tone, "Oh? Would you be in position to say just when, where, and with whom I last disgraced myself like this?"

She purred, "Who cares? She sure as hell didn't get it *all,* and I've got another interesting position to suggest as soon as we recover from that last one. I'm so glad that asshole picked my roof to shoot at you from, handsome. To think I might have gone to my grave without ever having been screwed right!"

He forced a chuckle he didn't feel. "Yeah, I've been wondering why he picked your roof in particular, Mame. What do you know about your neighbors to either side?"

"Not much. I don't go in for hen parties. I prefer the company of cocks."

"I noticed. Let's study on your neighbors anyway. I got a reason."

Mame yawned again. "Well, if you don't like *my* screwing, you won't like either of my neighbors, either. Rooming

48

house to the left is run by an old Irish woman who watches out her front window all day, saying her beads and trying to catch someone walking down the street with her skirts Rainy Suzy. I suspect she writes to the Pope every time she sees an ankle."

He nodded and said, "So much for any of the front doors along here, then. What about her roomers, honey?"

"Hell, I don't know any of 'em personal, handsome. They ain't the sort of natural-natured gal like me would want to know. She's got some day workers, like me, and a couple of old retired spinster gals who hardly ever go out, let alone enjoy life. Why?"

He patted her fondly. "That ain't the sort of rooming house a stranger would pick to sneak about in. What about the one down the other way? I noticed a cleaning gal in the hall as I dashed through."

Mame shrugged and said, "That figures. The old German gal who runs it even scrubs down her front steps every morning."

"Then there'd be no telling when someone might or might not meet someone else in the hall next door. Yeah, I reckon *I'd* have chosen this place, too, no offense."

The brassy blonde pouted and asked, "Are you calling me a sloppy housekeeper, you mean thing?"

"Just a mite more casual than either of your doubtless fussy neighbors, honey," he soothed.

"Well, I'll have you know there's more than one rooming house on this same block that ain't kept fit for pigs!"

"I don't doubt you. But how many buildings at all on this side of the street offer such a clear shot at the main entrance of the federal building across the way? I can see why the rascal with the buffalo gun chose your roof, now. All that's left is how he knew to. To a stranger just riding up the alley out back, one rooming house would have looked as good as any other. You say you hire rooms to transients, Mame. When's the last time a new roomer checked in and, more important, was he dressed cow?"

She thought, then said, "I haven't had anyone checking in this month. Come to think of it, the last time I took on a new roomer was almost three months ago, and he's a barkeep at the Parthenon, not a cowhand. Only man living here who leaves for work in boots and jeans is a gent called Gimpy, working down in the Burlington yards."

Longarm swore softly and said, "I know him. He ain't much, but I can't see him as a gunslick. I'll be switched if I don't think I could be sniffing at the wrong hole. I have to get back across the street, pronto. Just thought of something."

"Oh, hell, I was looking forward to getting excited again. Can't we come at least one more time before you go?"

He knew he could spend more time arguing with a brassy blonde in heat than it would take to pleasure her. So he gallantly suggested one for the road. While he humped her, he stared out the window, feeling a little foolish as he watched fully dressed federal employees returning from lunch, across the way. One of the gals he noticed going up the granite steps was Penny Wiggins, of all people, alone, with her trim back unguarded, curse Billy Vail's hide!

The brassy blonde responded to his uninspired but workmanlike thrusts to shudder in orgasm and fall away from him moaning, "Oh, God, I've never come so many times with one man before!"

Longarm commenced to haul on his duds. Mame rolled over to catch him at it, sighing, "Oh, are you leaving so soon? Listen, I could always go on a diet if you want to make this a steady lunch break, lover!"

He smiled down at her as he buttoned up, saying, "I like you just the way you are, you cute little thing. As to when I may or may not have lunch with you again, I'll be out in the field a spell. But it's always nice to know there's a candle burning in the window for me right across the street."

"Pooh! I know your rep. I'll bet there's other, better-looking gals you spend your lunch hours with, right?"

"Now don't get pouty, Mame. The only gal I know well enough to have lunch with regular, lives all the way up on Sherman Avenue. We'll talk about it later, hear?"

He chuckled his way across to the federal building and marched into Billy Vail's office. His superior glared up at him and said, "You sure took your own sweet time getting back here to apologize. Does that blonde have a friend who admires older men?"

Longarm saw that his badge still lay where he'd dropped it. So he picked it up and put it away, saying, "When you're right you're right. I'm off to Montana. The B.I.A. asked for me personal, right?"

"Yeah, they said you could call a meeting of the Black-foot leaders and . . . What are you looking so smug about, old son? A minute ago you were saying you'd resign before you'd go!"

"That was before I realized someone didn't want me to. Both them gunslicks I tangled with was wearing new American-style cow duds. Both wore their new hats creased Montana. Neither one tried for Miss Penny Wiggins, and she's littler than me. So the attempts on me had nothing to do with the old railroad-robbing case down here in the States. At least two old boys from Canada don't *want* me to settle the beef betwixt the Blackfoot and the Plains Cree. So I'd best get up there pronto and find out why."

Vail stared at him unwinkingly as he digested what Long-arm had said. Then he nodded sagely. "By God, that works. Up to a point. But why would Canadian *white* men be worried about you stopping a war between U. S. and Canadian Indians?"

Longarm said, "Don't know. I'll ask as soon as I catch

51

the next one. If they're gunning for me, the sooner I'm on my way, the sooner everyone here in Denver can breathe easier. Where the hell is your prissy clerk with my travel orders?"

Vail glanced at the banjo clock and said, "Dentist. He should be back in about half an hour."

Longarm nodded. "That gives me time for a couple of drinks at the Parthenon, and I surely deserve 'em. You've no idea how hard I have to work for this outfit, Billy."

"You call what I'm sure you just did to that fat blonde across the street *work?*" Vail laughed.

Longarm left, saying, "It is when they're that fat and a man has more important things on his mind."

Outside, he reconsidered. It was true he had time for a couple of drinks. But now that he was sure old Mame was innocent he remembered, wistfully, that he'd never even come in her that last time, and needled beer wasn't about to do as much for a redawning erection as a sassy, willing blonde even closer than the damned saloon could.

On the other hand, he'd already said adios, and parting was more a pain in the ass than the sweet sorrow some called it. He decided he'd best quit while he was ahead.

He kept his innocence halfway down the hall. Then Penelope Wiggins popped out an office door at him like a cuckoo sounding one P.M. and said, "Custis, we have to talk!" So he followed her inside.

He knew this particular office well, having spent some time in it, aboard another lady, aboard the leather chester-field against the wall. It was still furnished and occasionally cleaned layout leftover from a defunct branch of the B.I.A. It said right on the door that this was where one went to inquire about Indian affairs on a nearby Arapaho reservation. But since the War Department had taken over the reserve for a training camp, the only affairs taking place in here were between federal employees who knew the office was empty and forgotten by the powers that be.

Longarm left it up to her whether the door got locked or not. She must have wanted to keep the conversation quiet, since she turned the latch behind them as she said, "I ran into your clerk, Henry, at lunch."

Longarm said, "Do tell? He's supposed to be at the dentist. But I reckon he's been working here long enough to know the ropes. Old Billy expects us to eat in half an hour unless we have a good excuse."

"Never mind about them," she said. "Henry said they're sending you off on a field assignment and that there's no telling when you'll be back. I tried to get him to tell me where, but he said it was an official secret."

"Yeah, old Henry is sort of officious. But it ain't no mystery, honey. I got to go up to Montana and powwow with some Indians. As to when I'll be back, I'll be back as soon as I can, for you're prettier than any Blackfoot I've met so far."

As he took her in his arms to prove it she tried to back away, flustered. "Stop it! It's broad day and we're supposed to be at work, you big goof!"

He hung on gently until they wound up with her backed against the window, the broad sill against her tailbone. "What did you invite me in here for, if you didn't want me to start, Penny?"

She spread her feet to brace herself as she felt her back against the hopefully secure sash window and, as she could feel what was pressing against her open lap through all those layers of cloth between them, she giggled despite herself. "One would have thought you'd had enough of me last night!"

He said, "Honey, no matter how much one gets, it's never enough."

He kissed her. She kissed back.

But when they came up for air she insisted, "Behave yourself. What I wanted to tell you was that I had time to think after you left my place last night and I think we behaved very foolishly."

He nodded soberly and replied, "It sure looks foolish, when you watch *others* doing it."

She grimaced. "My, what a romantic way you have with words! But, all right, if we have to discuss earthy matters in earthy terms, we behaved like barnyard stock last night, and I'm still trying to figure out what came over me!"

He started moving his bulging fly in the interesting crease of her summer skirts as he soothed, "Nothing came over you, or in you, that wasn't natural to human or other critters, honey. But I've woke up in some cold gray dawns, too. Are you trying to say this office romance strikes you as indiscreet?"

She sighed and thrust her pelvis against him harder as she replied, "I certainly thought so when I brought you in here to call it off! I thought you'd have seen things the same way, once you cooled down, but, heavens, you don't seem to have cooled down very much, darling!"

He didn't think it polite to explain how he'd just been reinspired across the street by another, albeit less nicely built, gal. He didn't think, in fact, this was a time to explain anything. So he kissed her some more to end the dumb conversation as he reached down to haul her skirts up around her waist. She was wearing silk drawers, damn her, but fortunately they were loose as well as silky.

As she grasped his intent she rolled her lips aside to protest feebly, "Are you crazy? We're right against the window!"

He just unbuttoned his fly, got his raging erection out, and moved the crotch of her drawers out of the way as he

54

assured her, "What can anyone see from down below?"

She gasped, "No, wait!" as he entered her with her buttocks pressed half sitting on the sill and started moving in her hard. For the cool, distracted practice with the brassy blonde had surely gotten his glands working right again. Penny threw her arms around him, if only to keep from crashing out the window backwards, and moved her own body wildly in either a futile attempt to reject his advances or, more likely, from the way she started bumping and grinding in time with him, with considerable enjoyment. She came, in fact, ahead of him, but not by more than a very few strokes. For the contrast between a plump, naked blonde and a fully dressed petite brunette in less than an hour would have been inspiring enough even if he'd really let himself go with old Mame across the street.

Having warmed this one up again, Longarm reached down to grab a thigh on either side and carry her to the chesterfield without withdrawing, as Penny clung to him, giggling and wiggling, as she begged him not to drop her.

He didn't, and it was even better on the padded leather with her high-button shoes locked across the nape of his neck, although their clothes, his hat, and his gun rig not only got in the way but made her laugh like hell. He suggested they strip down and do it right, pointing out that the door was locked. But she signed and said, "I can't, damn it. Officially, I just stepped out to the ladies' room, and they're going to wonder why I took so long as it is. I have to get back to the pool, and . . . could you move a little faster, dear?"

He did. It was easy. But he had a train to catch, too. So when they finished climaxing again he said, "Well, I'll have mercy on you for now. Figure on me getting back from Montana in less'n a week, hear?"

She didn't answer until they were both sitting up and

smoothing down their somewhat rumpled duds. Then she shook her head and said, "Don't rise until I slip out. And don't say anything, damn it, until I'm finished this time."

He nodded silently. She said, "Obviously I can't resist you. I told you last night how weak-natured I am. But I value my reputation and I need this job. So, please, can't you be strong for both of us, dear?"

She'd told him not to say anything, so he didn't. She went on, "I don't want you to look me up when you get back, Custis. I mean, I *want* you to, too much by far! But I don't want to be involved with anyone where I work, and . . . Oh, I don't know *what* I want! You'll have to be strong and sensible for both of us, Custis!"

He nodded and said, "You'd best go, then, Miss Penny. What just happened never happened, if that's the way you want it."

"I *thought* it was the way I wanted it." She sighed and added, "I thought, last night, you'd just been using me as one of your many love toys, and I brought you in here resolved to end our relationship for good. But you were so . . . so virile and . . . You must really want me more than I thought, right?"

He chuckled fondly and said, "I sure don't *hate* you, honey. But you asked me to be strong and sensible. So you'd best get going before my weak nature gets the better of us again."

She got to her feet, but said, "Maybe we can talk about it some more when you get back from Montana. Maybe by then we'll both have our feelings under control."

He doubted that, but he agreed and, as he lit a smoke in gentle dismissal, she left. He felt so good about that he almost laughed out loud. For she'd been right as rain about office romances, and he'd been wondering how on earth he was going to end theirs gracefully.

Thanks to her practical she-male nature, the problem was solved.

At least until he got back from Montana.

Chapter 5

The first time Longarm had caught the train north to the Blackfoot country along the Canadian border he had enjoyed the long haul more, thanks to a pretty Blackfoot breed named Gloria. He had fibbed gallantly to Penny when he had said he'd never met a Blackfoot half as pretty as she was. But this time he couldn't pick up even an ugly gal on the infernal train. All he got to do was look out at the scenery, which stayed much the same for mile after tedious mile. Once they'd passed Billings, the miles passed more slowly, for the tracks got more twisty as well as more casually laid. There wouldn't have been any rails at all had not the Great White Father, in a moment of absent-minded fairness, told the rail barons that they couldn't have all those land grants for more profitable rights-of-way unless they served post offices and Indian agencies even where civilization thinned out a mite.

A million years after Longarm left Denver, they dropped him off with his saddle, Winchester, and possibles on an open railroad platform surrounded by nothing but lots of nothing as far as the eye could see. It felt even more lonesome after the train had chugged off. Billy Vail had told Longarm they were expecting him at the Indian agency, but the closest thing to a welcoming committee seemed to be a redwing cursing him from the telegraph wires overhead.

Longarm consulted his pocket watch. The train hadn't brought him here early. He'd arrived almost forty-five minutes late. But, as he gazed hopefully around, he saw nothing but rolling summer-killed prairie and, way the hell off to the west, a jagged purple streak that had to be the Lewis Range of the Rockies. He sat down on the sun-silvered planking with his boots in the buffalo grass and his left elbow braced atop his McClellan and saddle roll as he fished out a cheroot and lit it. When a man found his fool self on an Indian reservation he had to try to think like an Indian, and few Indians thought much of the way white men kept time.

Indians, despite cruel remarks to the contrary, were tolerable at keeping track of the time their own way. They never, for instance, went hungry just because a white man's tick-tock said it wasn't supper time yet. They knew better than any calendar when a hunter might find meat migrating, and which way. They knew when it was time to get up, go to bed, or hold a medicine dance. They just found it hard to grasp that white folk meant the little hand pointed at one scribble and the big hand pointed at another scribble when they agreed to meet you someplace. Had Billy's wire said Longarm would arrive when the shadows of the telegraph poles were starting to stretch out across the grass to the east, but before the gnats commenced to swarm, there would have been a buckboard from the agency waiting for him.

Despite the way the prairie rolled much the same all around, Longarm was getting his bearings back as he sat there smoking patiently. He had avoided getting off at the white settlement of Switchback this time. It would have been handier, since he could have hired a mount to put under this fool saddle at the more regular rail stop, but he hadn't been sent up here to talk to white folk and, more important, any white gunslicks wearing brand-new American hats who didn't want him talking to the Indians would be expecting him to detrain at Switchback. That was why he'd asked Billy to ask the Indian police to meet him here, more privately.

But where in thunder were the fool Indian police? Billy had told him his old Blackfoot friend, Rain Crow, was still in charge of them and, while Rain Crow thought Indian, he was still a federal peace officer who had to have some notion of the way a clock worked. Could someone have made a mistake about where he'd be getting off? The train would have pulled into Switchback by now, so he still had a chance of avoiding a night on the lone prairie. Old Rain Crow was smart. Once he noticed that nobody answering Longarm's description got off at Switchback, it likely wouldn't take him all night to figure out where to look instead.

The redwing buzzed down at him again. Longarm muttered, "Aw, shut up, bird. I ain't fixing to settle on your range permanent." And then, though he knew better, Longarm stood up to have another look down the tracks toward the trail town over the horizon where the tracks ran together to a point. He told the redwing, "I reckon I could walk it before darkness falls total. But let's study on this. It has to be a good twelve miles, and that saddle ain't made of feathers. The agency I really want to get to is . . . shit, at least fifteen miles over *that* way. And I'd get caught sure by sundown trudging my weary way west. You're right, bird. I'd best stay put instead of acting like an itchy white man. I'd look a total fool if I was nowhere at all in tricky light on rolling range when they come for me from either direction."

He sat back down. His smoke was done for. He snuffed the short stub out on the planks and didn't light another. He'd brought along plenty of cheroots, having smoked what Indians called tobacco more than once, but it was too easy to keep track of the time counting butts. He'd just sit tight and, hell, if worse came to worst, he hadn't brought his bedroll just to keep his army saddle from blowing away in the evening breeze. He had a water bag and field rations, too. It hardly seemed possible he'd be stuck here more than a night, for he could always flag the morning train into Switchback and do it the less sneaky and easier way.

The redwing buzzed again and flew away, still complaining. Longarm frowned, got back to his feet, and stared about to see why. A pair of riders were coming at him alongside the tracks to the north. He nodded and muttered, "It's about time." Then, as he stared harder, he added softly, "What the hell?" For his welcoming committee, if that was what he was looking at, had seen fit neither to bring along a buckboard nor a spare mount for him to ride. It got even more mysterious when one considered both were riding white and that, if they weren't wearing pink Stetsons, which hardly seemed likely, the red sun above the mountains to the west was shining on mighty white hats.

New ones.

Longarm dropped casually off the platform, knelt in the grass, and saw that, sure enough, he couldn't see them coming now. Before he could, he drew his saddle gun from its scabbard and rolled under the platform.

Naturally, no grass grew under the well-weathered but solid planking, so Longarm had nearly a yard of clearance between the bare, dusty soil and the overhead planks and timbers. He crawled to the north end with his Winchester and levered a round in its chamber as he peered out. The dry grass blocked his view some, but screened him even better as he waited until, sure enough, the two riders reined in, just their heads and shoulders visible to Longarm as one said, "Hey, where in the hell did he go?"

Longarm wasn't sure he wanted to tell them until he knew them better. So he just lay tar baby as the other replied, "Beats the shit out of me! I told you he must have suspected something when he dropped out of sight like that. But how far could even a long-legged moose like Longarm run so sudden? You suppose he could have made that rise to the south running crouched over?"

His comrade replied, "No, but he must have, since there's no cover at all this side of it. What say you swing east across the tracks whilst I take that rise direct?"

"Hold it! See that McClellan there? He lit out with his saddle gun! Chasing Longarm over the skyline could get a man hurt, Ontario. If he's playing possum just over the rise with a Winchester in his delicate paws, we'd better restudy our options!"

The one called Ontario spat and said, "Hell, we was sent to get him. Let's *get* him! The boss never told us he'd be easy. But that's why they pay gents like us so well."

Longarm had heard enough. The problem was how he aimed to just wing at least one of them when all he could see to aim at was their infernal heads and shoulders. He gathered his legs under him, drew a bead on the one who talked less boastfully, since he figured to be more dangerous, and blew the side of his head off before he popped out from under the platform, levering another round in his saddle gun while he roared, "Grab sky or die, you son of a bitch!"

Ontario must have thought he was as good as he talked, for he aimed the pistol he'd already drawn at Longarm instead. They both fired at the same time. Longarm grimaced in disgust as Ontario rolled backward out of his saddle to injure himself further by landing across one steel track on the small of his back with a grisly crunch. The two ponies he'd rid of their riders took off in either direction as the tall deputy moved in to survey the damage, levering another .44-40 round in the chamber.

It was just force of habit. Neither of the rascals needed another bullet in him at the moment. The one he'd hit in the head lay sprawled in the grass like a discarded rag doll, oozing blood and brains. The one he'd hoped to take alive

62

wasn't in much better shape as he lay staring in bewilderment at the sky with a punctured lung and a broken back. But his lips still twitched and his eyes kept blinking, so Longarm hunkered down on the railroad ballast beside his head and said, "Howdy. Didn't your mama ever tell you it ain't smart to fire a pistol against a rifle at medium range, Ontario?"

The dying gunslick murmured, "Who turnt out the lights? I can't *see* nothing, durn it!"

Longarm said, "That's generally the first thing as goes, Ontario. But hearing lasts a mite longer. So I'm asking you to tell me, just for the record, how come the two of you was after me."

Ontario told him to go to hell. Longarm said, "I may, in time. But you figure to be waiting for me there, old son. I'm sorry I killed you. I meant to take you alive. But that's the way things go sometimes. I can see why you could be feeling surly towards me right now, but it's to your advantage to offer me some information anyway. For one thing, I could see they spelled your name right on your grave marker. For another, I could even see you got buried on your home grounds, if you'd like to tell me where we should ship your remains."

Ontario grimaced and barely managed to whisper, "Fuck you, Longarm!"

Longarm chuckled fondly. "This ain't no time for us to flirt, old son. I doubt like hell you boys come all the way down from Canada to enjoy my fair white body. Who sent you after me, and why?"

No answer.

Longarm insisted, "I don't have no enemies in Canada. No living ones, leastways. You can't be working for the Canadian government, ornery as it feels about us right now. It's got something to do with Indians, right?"

63

Still no answer. Longarm swore, reached out to close Ontario's dead eyes, and patted the body down. He opened the wallet he found and growled, "Have it your way. *Brown* is the name we'll bury you under, you mysterious son of a bitch."

The other body had a wallet in a hip pocket, but no attempt at identification at all. Longarm removed the modest cash from both wallets before throwing them as far away as he could. As they vanished in the grass on the far side of the tracks he mused aloud, "We wouldn't want to confuse my office with tedious discussions of empty wallets, would we?"

One of the ponies the gunfire had spooked was nowhere to be seen now. The other, made of sterner stuff, or lazier, was grazing a few yards south along the tracks where the grass grew a little greener in the ditch. Longarm put the Winchester on his saddle as he passed the platform and called out soothingly, "I want a word with you, horse. Your friend likely run for Switchback. I don't want to be here when any friends of your recent rider come out here to find out why. So you and me are going over to the Blackfoot agency, right?"

The buckskin gelding eyed him warily, moved off a few yards, and then, as Longarm stood still, lowered its muzzle to the grass again. Longarm said, "I know, pard. They feed you shameless in that Switchback livery stable them gun-slicks must have hired you from since, no offense, you sure don't look like anything *I'd* ride all the way from Canada. Why don't you and me just ride over to the agency and see if they have some nice yummy oats for you, hear?"

The gelding, of course, had no idea what Longarm was talking about, but as the experienced plainsman hoped, the oft-mistreated livery mount was soothed by his gentle if inane conversation. As he worked his way closer, Longarm said, "Easy does it, old timer. You can see you can't graze decent with your reins dragging in the grass like that. So I'd best sort of reach down—easy, now—and pick 'em up for you, see?"

He got both reins before the buckskin could reconsider and try to dance off again. The dancing stopped suddenly when Longarm gave the reins a gentle but firm tug. "Fun's over, you useless old crowbait," he told the animal. "We're going to go get my saddle now. We'll leave the one they hired along with you here, for now. I sure wish the bastard as hired you in Switchback had rid out on his own. If you had saddlebags I could search 'em, but you don't, so we'll say no more about 'em."

He led the nag over to his own possibles, tethered him to one platform leg, and switched saddles, giving the buckskin a friendly rubdown with its own sweaty saddle blanket before tossing it aside and replacing it with his own clean, dry one. The buckskin was already feeling more friendly to him by the time he and the McClellan were aboard and they were headed west into the gathering dusk.

They rode a good two miles toward the agency before, topping a rise, Longarm spied company coming their way against the blood-red western sky. He drew his saddle gun again, thoughtfully. The motion was not wasted on the Indian police chief, Rain Crow, who called out, "Is that you, Longarm? Here speaks a friendly person, Rain Crow. We brought buckboard. But I see you already got pony. I am sorry we are so late. Have we kept you waiting long?"

As the four riders and buckboard came into easier speaking range Longarm put his Winchester away. "I notice you boys was taking your time this evening," he said. "But I found things to occupy my time while I waited. As you see, I don't need a buckboard ride. But two white men I left over by the tracks sure do. I just shot 'em. Seeing as how

65

we have transportation now, I'd like to take 'em along to the agency with us. I'll show you the way, since you've obviously been having trouble finding that old railroad platform this evening."

Rain Crow said, "Wait. My young men can fetch the bodies for us. You and I had better get back to the agency fast, Longarm. We were not late because we did not know where you were or when you'd be there. We have had more trouble. Big trouble. The elders are waiting at the agency to see what our white brother wants to do about it. We don't want to keep them waiting. They are already crying blood."

Longarm nodded soberly. "We'd best get cracking, then. What happened, Rain Crow?" he asked.

The Indian peace officer said, "Plains Cree. This time they took hair. This time means war. Never scalp a Blackfoot if you don't want a war!"

Chapter 6

The council fire was burning on the flat, sandy bottom of a dry wash a short ride or a long walk from the agency settlement itself. As Longarm and Rain Crow took the places saved for them to the left of the presiding chief, Longarm saw that he was the only white invited. He understood enough of their Algonquinoid dialect to get the feeling more than one old cuss seated around the fire didn't think *he* should be there, either. In case his Blackfoot was rusty, one hawk-faced old bastard drew an imaginary hatband across his own forehead in the universal High Plains sign for a white man and added a particularly obscene gesture as he growled, "Hear me, this is not the time we should petting the flea-bitten dogs of Wa-shung-ting!"

Longarm didn't answer. Nobody had spoken to him directly. He figured somebody would sooner or later. Meanwhile the mostly old men gathered around the fire were an interesting study in what was wrong with Uncle Sam's current Indian policy.

The Indian policeman to his left was, of course, dressed white, save for the quillwork band of his high-crowned black hat. The old chiefs were trying to look more Indian, with ancient regalia over their agency-issue denim and calico. The wrinkled old buzzard who'd called the council wore a prairie-elk-hide shirt trimmed in white weasel and real quillwork that probably belonged in a museum. His name, as Longarm recalled, was Snake Killer. He wasn't called that because he stomped on rattlers. In his younger days he'd killed more Shoshone, or Snake Indians, than anyone else could remember. The last time they'd met, old Snake Killer had calmed down some and, aside from believing more in Medicine than Longarm, could be considered reasonable, for a Blackfoot.

The people the white man called Blackfoot only called themselves that when they were speaking English, of course. Like most Native Americans, their own term for themselves was "People" or "Us." In the case of this particular group the term was "Piegan," meaning something more like "Real Men." But old Snake Killer must not have wanted to hear a visiting white man's attempt at his own lingo, for he spoke English as he stared soberly at Longarm and said, "My heart soars to see you still live, Longarm. The last time you came you saved the Blackfoot from the Wendigo. This time we are in real trouble. This time it is not Medicine. This time we face real war, with many enemies, many. You must tell the Great White Father to give us guns. Many guns. The dog-eating Cree have repeating rifles. Good ones. Stolen from the Red Coats of the Big Squaw Victoria!"

Longarm nodded soberly. "Hear me, I have been told this by others," he said. "I am trying to understand it. I have smoked with Plains Cree on the buffalo grounds of Canada. They, too, sing sad songs about their Shining Times. But the last time I saw them they were eating fat cow next to my Blackfoot brothers. I don't see why Cree would want to come down here when the Mounties still allow them more freedom than some of my own people in Washington think any Indian should have. I can't help wondering if we are talking about the same people. Isn't it possible the people bothering you could be from another nation? In the Shining Times my Blackfoot brothers counted coup on people closer to home. How do we know we are not talking about Assiniboin or Ojibwa? Why do we have to be talking about Cree, from fine hunting grounds to the north?"

An old man across the fire wailed, in English so Longarm would get the message in full, "Listen to the snapping puppy! Oh, by Manitou, I weep blood for the mother who bore such a stupid son, even if she was a white woman! Horse Bite is right! You never should have invited him to sit in council with real men! He does not know the difference between Assiniboin and Cree! He thinks *we* are stupid, too!"

Snake Killer waited politely until he'd calmed some before he replied softly, "He is young. He is wrong. But it makes me feel good to hear a white man with a badge think twice before he offers to shoot any kind of real person. Let us all be calm while I explain some things to my little white brother with good medicine."

Snake Killer reached behind him to haul forth a length of lodgepole pine with an improvised flag of white canvas nailed to it. He spread the cloth on the sand between him and Longarm, saying, "The Cree who was carrying this got away, wounded. Look at the design."

Longarm did. Someone had painted what looked like playing card diamonds on the canvas with what looked like cow or buffalo blood. Human blood would have dried to a browner shade. The design could stand for arrowheads, belly buttons, or even men, in the not-too-certain artistic conventions of the Plains Indian. He said, "I see a banner painted with blood. I don't see Cree written on it anywhere and, come to think on it, battle flags are a white man's notion."

Snake Killer fumbled out more evidence in the form of an odd war club. The head, instead of the solid wood or stone most Plains Indians favored, was a limp rawhide poke with a serious-sized rock inside it loose, so the weapon hit like an oversized blackjack instead of a mace. Longarm nodded. "That's a Cree war club for certain. Who counted coup on the man who carried it?" he asked.

An old man across from him looked pleased. "Hear me,

my sister's son, Little Moon, made a night raider drop that weapon and ride off without it," he said. "Hear me, Little Moon thinks he hit the enemy's pony, too!"

Longarm sighed. "If we're talking about the same young Little Moon, the last time I was up here he was learning to be a pretty good cowhand. I'd be proud of him if he was my nephew, too. But I sure wish we could get history to run forward instead of backward here."

Old Snake Killer smiled grimly and said, "Maybe it's your fault, to some extent, that our young men must act like men instead of cowboys, Longarm. Before you people got us to behave like whites, herding cows and even, damn it, growing crops, we did not have so much for others to steal. I think the Cree are mostly after our livestock. You must get us rifles, many repeating rifles. Can you do this for us, Longarm?"

"Hear me, it is not up to me," Longarm said. "I was sent up here to find out what was going on. So let's talk some more. Rain Crow, here, tells me these mystery raiders have taken more than cows. He says the raiders have been scalping people, too."

Snake Killer nodded grimly. "Two women and a boy, just today," he said. "They were out picking choke cherries, far from the agency, when they were jumped. That is another reason we know we are at war with Cree. When a Blackfoot wants to sing his brag he does not carry on like a Cree or Teton about the hair he's lifted. We are serious people. We would rather boast of guns, horses, and women we have won in battle. If a real man kills an enemy in a good fight, and strikes his body with his bare hand before the dead enemy's friends can recover it, what does it matter if the disgraced enemy still wears his hair or not? But Cree are not like us. They feel undressed unless they have lots of scalps sewn to their shirts. They are very disgusting people. Sometimes they even divide a scalp to make it look like two and, of course, a woman's or even a child's scalp looks much like a real man's, sewn to a shirt. We Blackfoot all have beautiful hair."

Longarm frowned thoughtfully and said, "Assiniboin don't value scalps beyond common sense, neither. That does narrow it down some. Ojibwa have been known to lift she-male hair, but they don't hit hardly anyone with Cree war clubs."

Snake Killer nodded. "I am happy to see you thinking like a real person at last, Longarm," he said. "Now that you know why we are at war, let us all decide calmly what to do about it."

He produced a beautifully worked parfleche and reverently removed a calumet and other sacred objects. Everyone else fell silent lest they offend the spirits. The bowl of the calumet was carved from the soft green pipestone the Blackfoot considered better medicine than the red other nations favored. The long stem was festooned with strings of white weasel fur, elk teeth, bear claws, and the whole dried wing of a prairie owl. A greenhorn might have assumed the results were a so-called peace pipe. Longarm knew better. In the first place, there was no such thing as a peace pipe unless an Indian was using a calumet to smoke peace with. In the second place, the owl was the messenger of death and the bear, of course, stood for war.

Snake Killer spread a calico kerchief on the sand in front of him and placed a black dried buffalo tongue on it. Then he placed the bowl of the calumet on the tongue and began to stuff it with black tobacco as he explained, for Longarm's ears alone, "Hear me, this is real tobacco, grown by the Dream Society and never watered by any woman. It has no cherry bark in it. It is real."

He removed a peeled willow wand from his medicine bag and poked it into the fire to light the calumet. He puffed exactly seven times to get it going. Then he held the calumet in both hands and raised it high to show to the stars as he sang softly in his own lingo for a spell. Longarm wished he were somewhere else. For, naturally, once the stars had approved, old Snake Killer took the first serious drag on the calumet and then passed it to his left, to Longarm.

Longarm held the calumet respectfully as if it had been a lit stick of dynamite, but said, "I am here as a friend. I respect your traditions. That is why I can't smoke your sacred calumet with you yet."

There was a collective hiss of indrawn breath. At least two dozen pairs of ink-black eyes stared at him. The one old man who growled, "Kill him!" said it in his own lingo, but Longarm got the message.

As he'd sure hoped, the wise old Snake Killer stared stone-faced at him and asked, "Do you have a reason for insulting us so, Longarm?"

Longarm nodded. "If I didn't respect you all as men, not children to be humored, I'd just take my puff and pass it on. But that would mean I'd made a promise I'm not ready to make yet. Do I have to tell old men as wise as you all how bad it is for a white man to make an easy promise he's not sure he'll be able to keep?"

A middle-aged man across the circle got to his feet and, since he must have wanted Longarm to understand, sang in English even though it didn't rhyme:

"Hear me! I am Wolf Eyes!
    I am of the Kit-Fox Lodge.
        I was born to die fighting.
            If there is anything hard to do I will do it.
                If there is anything dangerous to do I will
                    do it.

72

I am not afraid to die.
I piss on those afraid to die.
Only cowards die of old age.
And I am not a coward.
I have spoken!"

Longarm listened politely until Wolf Eyes sat back down, still alive and a lot older than him, before he said, still holding the calumet unsmoked, "I have no death song prepared. I may well be a coward. Or I may just want to wait until I see who I have to fight before I make any promises to my spirits or your own. I just got here. I still don't know what's going on. When I do, I'll do something about it."

Snake Killer cut in, which was impolite for an Indian, so Longarm knew the old chief was seriously upset as he insisted, "Longarm, we have lost cows. We have lost horses. We have lost *hair!* We thought you were our friend!"

"I think I am, too," Longarm said. "That's why I'm trying to talk straight to you instead of showing off. Do you remember the last time I was up this way, when an earlier chief asked for help, Snake Killer?"

Snake Killer nodded, but said, "Please don't mention the name of one who no longer walks the earth. We know who you are speaking of. He was a good chief. Better than me. The Wendigo killed him before you got here. But then you killed the Wendigo. *That* time you made *sense!*"

Longarm smiled thinly. "That time you all were talking mighty dumb, too. The killer you all had down as He-Who-Walks-the-Sky-at-Night was a human being, hired by white men who were out to steal your land. While you were looking for him in the night sky, I studied on how to catch the son of a bitch with his feet and mind on the solid ground. You all may have noticed, I *caught* him, too. So before I light out after anyone else around here, I mean to investigate

73

some. That's what you call my kind of hunting, investigating."

He handed the unsmoked calumet back to the old man, who protested, "What are we supposed to do in the meantime? Wait like women to be killed and scalped?"

Longarm said, "Of course not. You have your Indian police here, and if some of your young men want to be deputized as more of the same, I can see it's done lawfully. You have the same constitutional right as anyone else to defend your lives and property. Should anyone, red or white, come at anyone on this reserve again, I'll back you to the limit if you gun the son of a bitch. But meanwhile I want everyone to sit tight, stay inside the reservation lines, and go easy on the feathers and paint. In case you've forgotten, there's an army post less than a day's ride from here and, once a green officer fresh from the East hears tales of wild Indians on the warpath, there's just no telling what he might do."

Another old Indian bawled, "Why don't the Blue Sleeves go after those damned Cree if they're so anxious to fight real people?"

Longarm said, "I mean to ask 'em. I mean to ask lots of questions of lots of people. No offense, but nothing I've heard yet makes sense!"

"You shouldn't have made the old ones so mad at you," said Rain Crow as he rode with Longarm toward the agency headquarters. "Now they won't like you as much."

Longarm shrugged as they topped another rise to see pinpoints of light ahead. "I wasn't sent up here to win no popularity contests," he replied. "I was sent to see if I could stop a war, and it looks like I got here just in time."

"No, you didn't," Rain Crow said. "The fighting has already started."

"Yeah, but so far it's defensive, on the Blackfoot side, at least. One out of two ain't bad. Where are these so-called

Cree camped right now, Rain Crow?"

The Indian snorted in disgust. "If we knew that, do you think we'd be asking for help? If we knew where they were coming from, we'd just go there, and they'd never come from there again. You are right about one thing. We need a good tracker. And I'll never forget how you tracked the Wendigo across the starry sky that time, Longarm."

Longarm started to say again that he'd done no such thing, but the trouble with folk who believed in spooks was that you couldn't get them to stop believing in spooks. Rain Crow was better educated than most of his people and Longarm had thought he'd explained that other case to him well enough for a child to understand. But maybe Rain Crow *needed* to have spooks haunting him. Lots of white folk did, though they gave their own spooks different names. To change the subject, he asked Rain Crow, "Is the agent we're riding to meet still Cal Durler?" and the Indian said, "No. He had what the white medicine men call a nervous collapse shortly after you left. We have a new agent called Crimmins now. He is older. He makes more sense than the weakling we had before. The trader and his wife are new, too. He's a Metis named Chambrun, married to a Miami woman who prays to Jesus in the fashion of the Black Robes. They are good people. He is only half white, so he knows how to trade with us right."

Longarm frowned thoughtfully as he mused, half to himself, "A Red River breed and a Catholic Miami, eh? Do you know if this Chambrun's a U. S. citizen, Rain Crow?"

Rain Crow nodded and said, "He is now. He used to be Canadian. But of course the B.I.A. only issues trading licenses to U. S. citizens. I don't know what you call his wife. She's a full blood, like me. So I guess she doesn't get to drink liquor either. Do you mind if I ask you something, Longarm? Why is it that breeds and colored people are allowed to vote and drink, while we are not?"

Longarm sighed. "I've never figured that out, neither. If it's any comfort to you, there's places colored folk ain't allowed to vote, either. Though, come to think on it, they can *drink* all they like, as long as it's not right next to an unreconstructed rebel or a Union vet who's sort of forgot what the War was all about. Could we stick to race relations closer to here? How've you Blackfoot been getting along with the neighboring white settlers and the folks in Switch-back lately?"

"As well as we can expect to with people who stole most of Montana Territory from us. You said you'd cleaned out those evil whites who were trying to steal more of our land that time, didn't you?"

"Yeah. It's my fond hope they've stayed cleaned out. But it's one of the angles I'll have to look into. Aside from Indians pestering you and yourn, I've been having more trouble than usual with white men of late. It's sure funny how often I've tripped over white men mixed up in your Indian uprisings, Rain Crow. Up to now it's never been misplaced patriotism, either. But I'll be switched if I can figure how the meanest Canadian birthed to mortal woman could hope to profit by this latest outbreak. How many head of livestock have you all lost, so far?"

Rain Crow thought and said, "Maybe thirty cows. We watch our horses better. Why?"

"There goes cattle rustling for fun and profit. Thirty head is a lot to lose, but hardly enough to enter the beef industry with. Your cows are all marked with that big Interior De-partment brand, I hope?"

"Of course. The government brands them before we get them. We used to just slaughter them and eat them right away. But, partly thanks to you, we have enough young men who are willing to work as cowhands now."

They rode on for a time in silence. Then Rain Crow said, "I just thought of something. Up in Canada, the Cree have not learned to herd cattle yet. They still hunt their meat and, even in Canada, the buffalo are getting harder to find every summer. Everyone knows Cree eat dogs. Would a man who ate dogs taste much difference between a buffalo and a beef cow?"

"I follow your drift. You Blackfoot and the Plains Cree have never been on neighborly terms and, yeah, the notion of old enemies having a whole herd of beef on hand could make a disappointed buffalo hunter sort of wistful. But I was up Canada way not long ago and I *saw* buffalo, not far north of the border, as a matter of fact. There's a hunk of this puzzle missing, Rain Crow. If you were a Cree, would you want to risk a running gunfight, off your home range, with the U. S. whites and Indians combined, if all you wanted was a scrawny old cow your squaw couldn't even tan a decent robe from?"

"I don't know. I'm not a Cree, thank Manitou. It was crazy to kill women and children, too. But they *did* it!"

"*Somebody* did, you mean. I've been swapping lead of late with gents busting a gut to look like American cowhands. What's to stop some surly son of a bitch from acting like a Cree?"

Rain Crow shook his head and said, "The people raiding us have been Indians. Hear me, why should we suspect *other* Indians when everyone knows the Cree were our favorite enemies in the Shining Times?"

Longarm shook his own head and replied, "You mean you *think* you've been getting raided by other Indians, just like I'd have thought a gang of Americans was after me, if I wasn't so damn smart. Have you recovered a body? Has one of your young men gotten even close enough to count coup on one of the rascals?"

"Well, not exactly, but we've wounded at least a couple of them."

"There you go. Hell, I could hit a lady with a Cree war

77

club if I was feeling nasty and, if I got away, who'd know the difference?"

"You're speaking foolishly, even for a white man. Our young men don't shoot at targets they can't see, and they saw other Indians to shoot at!"

"In tricky light, riding lickety-split, mayhaps wearing Indian duds and furniture stain? I took in more'n one of them minstrel shows they hold in Denver in my time. You ever see a minstrel show, old son?"

"No. What is a minstrel show?"

"They lines up a whole mess of colored gents on the stage to play banjos and tell jokes about colored folk. Some of them are sort of silly. Only they ain't really colored men at all. They're white men wearing burnt cork and fuzzy wigs. To tell the truth, you can tell they're really white men if you look close, in the bright lighting they use. But at a distance, in poor light..."

"Heya, I like the funny stories you tell about the outside world, Longarm. But what about the scalps taken in broad daylight?"

"By a person or persons unknown." Longarm nodded. "Them cherry pickers weren't hit by daylight with anyone *watching*. As to white men knowing how to lift hair, the Mexican government used to pay a forty-dollar bounty on Apache scalps, and hardly anybody in the business was a paid-up Indian."

They were still arguing about it as they rode into the agency headquarters settlement, which consisted mostly of log and unpainted frame buildings wrapped about a central space trampled too bare to qualify as a village green. Longarm spotted a buckboard in front of the building he remembered as the Indian police station. As they rode over, one of the Indians Rain Crow had sent to fetch the trackside bodies was sitting on the steps. He got up and came forward, saying, "You must not have really killed anyone, Longarm. When we got there we found blood near the tracks. That was all. I think they must have gotten up and walked away after you left."

Longarm grimaced and said, "That hardly seems likely. One of their ponies ran back to town. Their pals must have beat you boys there by a whisker. They sure as hell never made it home on their own!"

Chapter 7

The sound of hoofbeats followed by a conversation in English had carried to the whitewashed quarters of the agent himself. He came outside and walked over to join them as Longarm and Rain Crow were dismounting. Rain Crow introduced them. Longarm couldn't shake until he'd tethered the borrowed buckskin. When he did, the agent, Crimmins said, "We've been wondering where you were, Longarm. There's a townee gal inside who says she'd like a word with you."

Longarm frowned. "Do tell?" He was half afraid to ask her name, since the only gal from Switchback he recalled lay six feet under last time he'd looked, and it sort of hurt to think about old Roping Sally and how she'd got there.

But the gal who barged out to meet them as they approached the agent's house was too small and spitfire-redhead to be the late Roping Sally and, come to study on it, too ornery. She strode up to him, hauled off, and slapped him across the face, yelling, "Steal *my* horse, will you, you no-good son of a bitch!"

He couldn't hit her back. He grabbed her wrists and hung on tight, surprised at her wiry determination. "Simmer down, Miss Whosomever!" he said soothingly. "If you're talking about a buckskin gelding, I never stole him. I rescued him from hired killers, and—"

"Bullshit!" she cut in. "My roan come back, lathered and mistreated. I rode out to see what happened. I met some Injun cusses poking about in the grass by the old flag stop.

I asked one of 'em where in the hell my buckskin was and he said you was last seen riding for this reserve with it. Can you deny you done the deed, you bastard?"

"Now you just simmer down before I wash your sassy mouth out with soap, missy!" he growled, still hanging on as he explained. "If anyone's in trouble here, it's you! I was riding your buckskin, if it's your buckskin, because I needed a ride and because I'd just shot a man off him that was out to shoot *me!* So hear my words and listen tight. You're talking to the federal law, and you'd best have a mighty good story if you don't aim to spend the night in the drunk tank across the way!"

She blanched but blustered, "You can't arrest me out here. I ain't no Indian!"

"Neither am I," he said. "So it sort of evens out. I'm still waiting to hear your tale, starting with who you are, Red."

She stopped struggling but still stared up at him defiantly as she replied, "I'm Bonnie Murphy. I owns the best durned livery stable in town, and you still owe me a buckskin gelding, mister!"

"Call me Custis now that we've stopped wrestling. You any kin to Sheriff Murphy in Switchback?"

"He's my uncle. What's it to you? Do you know him?"

"Yep. Worked with him on another case not long ago. He forgot to tell me he had a homicidal lunatic in his family, though. All right. You hire out horses. This afternoon you hired a roan and a buckskin to a couple of Canadians wearing white Stetsons, right?"

"I don't know if they was Canadians. They both spoke English. But you're right about the hats. You say you . . . *shot* 'em?"

"Had to. When I didn't get off the train at Switchback they rode out to gun me at the flag stop. I suspicion I saved

81

both of us some needless worry by gunning them instead, for I doubt they'd have come back with your mounts once I'd been killed."

She looked concerned enough for him to let go of her wrists. She rubbed them thoughtfully and said grudgingly, "Well, maybe I won't get my uncle to arrest you as a horse thief, after all. But you sure had me worried, Custis. I don't have that many durned old horses in the first place."

He knew it would be impolite to ask her if she was strapped for cash. It was obvious she was. He said instead, "Now that the war is over, Miss Bonnie, could I ask you just how much you charge a day for the use of a mount?"

"Two dollars a day, with you feeding, and of course a forty-dollar deposit afore you ride off. Why?"

"I ain't going to give you no deposit. You got to keep the forty on both, coming to eighty, thanks to me. But I do need a mount while I'm here, and the buckskin's a better one than he looks. So what say I hire him off you at a dollar a day and we'll settle up before I leave?"

"Damn it, you must have wax in your ears! Didn't you just hear me tell you my rates is *two* a day?"

"Sure, but I like a gal with a sense of humor. I'm only out to hire a mount, not to send your kids to college, Miss Bonnie. We both know a dollar a day is too steep. But I'm an agreeable cuss who can't resist red-headed women. So how's about it?"

She laughed despite herself and said, "Well, all right, but remember, all you're getting is the use of my buckskin. You can keep sassy remarks about my hair to yourself, hear?"

They shook on it and Crimmins heaved a sigh of relief. "I'm glad that's settled. You're just in time for coffee and cake, Longarm. You, too, Miss Bonnie. Let's go inside and tell my woman how much we admire her cooking." To his credit, Crimmins added, "That includes you of course, Rain Crow."

Rain Crow smiled pleasantly, but said, "No, thank you. It always makes your woman sick when I put flour in my coffee and, to tell the truth, I lose my appetite watching you people ruining it with sugar and cream. I have to post extra guards on the herd tonight, anyway."

As the Indian left, the others went inside. The front parlor had been repainted and looked more cheerful than Longarm remembered from the last time he'd been here. The former agent's wife, while a great little lay, had been a sort of casual housekeeper.

In the better light, Longarm saw that Crimmins was a man a little older than himself, but tanned and in good shape, save for a more bulging middle. His wife, Mary Lou, was even plumper, in a pretty way. She was one of those sweet little house-proud homemakers who started looking sort of motherly midway through their honeymoons and never seemed to change much till they were sweet little grand-mothers. From the way she smiled at everyone, old Crim-mins could have done worse. As she led them back to her kitchen and sat them down to partake of her coffee and fresh-baked chocolate cake, it was easy to see why the agent had the beginnings of a pot belly. Longarm had forgotten how long it had been since he'd eaten on that train until her down-home refreshments shocked his own belly awake. But he knew it wouldn't be polite to ask for more than second helpings. When they got up from the table to go back out to the parlor, his stomach was still growling despite two slices of cake and four cups of Arbuckle.

The agent's wife said she'd fixed up the guest room against his coming and that she hoped he'd find it com-fortable enough. She seemed surprised when he said he'd slept in it before, leaving out with whom. Her husband

83

laughed and said, "She never pays attention when I talk shop, Longarm. I told her you were the one who cleaned up that Wendigo case for the last agent. I'd sure like to hear the details of that one. It sounds mighty interesting."

Longarm grimaced. "To tell you the truth it was more gruesome than interesting—to ladies, at least—and it's ancient history as well."

He wanted to talk about the current troubles. But with two she-males sitting there staring at him like owl birds, he wasn't ready to discuss scalping techniques with a man who likely didn't have anything new to offer in any case. In fancier surroundings, it was customary for the womenfolk to go off and gossip in another room after everyone ate. But, while they'd fancied this shack up a mite since the last time he'd been there, it hadn't grown any extra rooms.

Somewhere in the house a clock chimed. Bonnie Murphy said, "Lord have mercy! I've stock to bed down in town. I'd best get going. I sure thank you for your fine refreshings, Mary Lou."

As she rose, Longarm rose, too, saying, "I'd best ride you into town then."

"What for?" the redhead asked. "It ain't far, and my paint's right out back."

"It's dark out, too. And I couldn't help noticing you ain't packing a gun, Miss Bonnie."

"I have a .22 varmint gun on my saddle."

"You still ain't packing a gun, then. So I'd best see you home safe."

Mary Lou looked concerned and said, "You're welcome to stay here tonight, Bonnie. There has been some trouble out here, you know."

Bonnie shook her head. "I'd like to. I can't. Like I said, I has to make sure my stock is secure for the night. I got a young stable boy on duty. But if I don't watch him, he reads Captain Billy Whizz Bang when he's supposed to be spreading bedding and such. Don't nobody worry about me. I rid out here in the dark. I can get home the same way."

Longarm shook his head as he followed her out. "You get your paint and I'll saddle the buckskin again," he said.

"Custis, this is silly. I'm a woman grown and . . . *That* ain't what you had in mind, is it?"

He shook his head soberly and replied, "One time, a million years and a funeral ago, another gal was riding alone on that same stretch of prairie and I'll never forgive myself. She was bigger than you, and wearing a sixgun as well. So let's not argue about it."

She tried to, being a woman, but in the end they were riding side by side in the moonlight. They were a couple of miles from the agency when a train whistled mournfully somewhere in the night. Bonnie gave a little gasp and said, "Of course. It was by the railroad tracks, further to the north. I remember now. That other gal was Roping Sally, wasn't she?"

"It was. Did you know her, Bonnie?"

"Not well. Used to see her around town, of course. She was a big, tough tomboy, ramrodded her own Lazy W spread, right?"

"Close enough. I don't like to talk about it, Bonnie. The Indians have a good notion about avoiding mention of the dead, when you study on it."

"Well, it is sort of owlhooty out here, so still and lonesome, with nary another soul for Lord knows how far. I don't mind saying right now your tagging along seems more comforting that I thought it would be back there where the light was brighter."

He said softly, "Be still. I'm trying to listen."

"Listen to what, Custis?"

"How in hell can I tell if you won't shut up and let me *listen?*"

"Oh, you're just horrid," she said. Then, before she could

85

say more, a ragged line of riders came over the rise to their north, yelling fit to bust as they charged at Longarm and Bonnie in the moonlight.

The redhead yelled, "Injuns!" and spurred her paint the other way. Longarm cursed, rode after her, and called out, "Not *that* way, you damned little fool!" Since there was no other way to stop her before she topped the next rise, he cursed again, drew his saddle gun, and blew her mount out from under her as he twisted his own mount's head around, threw his full weight the other way, and spilled it across the thick sod just as a bullet wizzed through the space they'd been filling with his form. He rolled free of the saddle as the buckskin went down, cussing in horse and trying to struggle back to its feet. But Longarm hauled it back down with a savage wrench of the reins and braced his Winchester across its heaving belly as he snapped, "Hey Bonnie! Get your ass over here on the double!"

Without waiting to see if she was following orders, Longarm fired at the mount, not the rider, of the nearest screaming Cree or whatever. The pony went down. Its rider was too slick to bounce right up, so all Longarm could do was blow some feathers away as the son of a bitch lay low behind his own mount. But Longarm's moonlight marksmanship had made the others rein in to reconsider, just out of easy rifle range.

Bonnie joined him behind the buckskin just as the rider he'd downed sprang up to run for it. He'd have never made it had not the redhead pounded both fists against Longarm's back as he fired, shouting, "You maniac! You just kilt my horse!"

"Shut up," he said. "If you hit me again I'll flatten you, too! You just made me miss an easy shot, you stupid little sass! If you want to be useful, keep your eyes peeled back the other way. You were about to ride into the oldest mistake in the book, and they may still hit us from that way."

She called him a maniac again, but turned to look back in the general direction of her own dead horse, at least. So when she gasped, "Oh, no!" Longarm just had to spin on his knees and fire upslope as the main party topped the rise to their south. Again he aimed for the mount and again it went down. But the son of a bitching rider managed to land rolling over the crest to safety, leaving only a lance driven into the sod near his dead pony.

Longarm said, "Nice going. Are you getting the way these things work, now?"

"They were trying to *trick* us!" she marveled. "They hoped we'd run into a sneaky ambush, trying to get away from the ones doing all the yelling, right?"

"You're learning. Can you handle a sixgun? Never mind. You have to. Haul my .44 off my hip. Then keep it trained on that lance up there. I don't know how to tell you this, but I only have eyes on one side of my fool head."

He turned to steady the Winchester north as he felt Bonnie draw his sidearm. He heard her cock it, so he didn't bother telling her how to shoot it. She was either a good shot or she wasn't. There was no way to teach her marksmanship at the moment.

As it turned out, she wasn't bad. Longarm flinched despite himself as his .44 went off right behind him. By the time he'd whirled again there was nothing upslope to shoot at, and Bonnie said, "Shit, I missed the fucker!"

He laughed. "You must have come close enough to scare him, anyway. We'd best trade places. It's starting to look like any further action we get will be from the south."

"I think I could make it to my own saddle gun, Custis. It's not far, and I can hit most anything with my old .22!"

He growled, "Will you just do as you're told for a change, Red? I want to *kill* the bastards, not *beesting* 'em!"

He grabbed her and swung her in place, with the pistol aimed across the buckskin to the north as he covered them from the rear with the Winchester.

"Why did you have to grab my tit just then, you brute?" she asked.

"Because I had to grab you somewheres and it was handy," he said. "Will you *please* keep your eyes on that rise to the north?"

"I am, I am, damn it, but nobody's coming at us from that way," she said.

"Well, don't fret about it, Red. You've only got four rounds in that gun now. Do you know how to reload a revolver?"

"Of course. Don't fuss at me. Give me the damned bullets!"

He laughed, reached in his coat pocket, and handed her some loose rounds. "Hang on to these. You're all right, Red. A mite stupid for such a willful child, but we might get out of this with our hair yet."

"If it looks like they're going to run us over, you'll shoot me before it's too late, won't you, Custis?"

He said, "If they don't do it first. Are you fixing to blubber up on me, funny face?"

"Hell, no! Powder River and let her buck! I ain't no sissy gal. I just don't want to die raped, if I can help it. How come it's so quiet all of a sudden? Do you reckon we run 'em off?"

"Not hardly, unless *they're* sissy gals. Wait a minute, I hear hoofbeats coming from the west. Unless we're about to go under, I think that's what's run 'em off."

It was. Rain Crow called out soon enough to avoid grisly accidents in the dark, and Longarm called back, "Watch your flanks, Rain Crow! We got 'em north and south of us!"

A few minutes later, after some scouting, Rain Crow and a dozen other agency Blackfoot rode in to tell Longarm he was wrong. One of them was carrying the lance from up on the south rise. The fluttering whiteness Longarm had taken in the dark for a bundle of feathers turned out to be another bloody banner painted in the same design. Rain Crow said, "Now maybe you will believe me when I say there are bad Indians around here! They were cowards, too! No real men would have let one man and one small woman drive them off!"

Longarm chuckled as he took his .44 back from Bonnie Murphy. "Oh, I don't know, Rain Crow," he said. "You ain't tangled with this one yet."

Chapter 8

The buckskin was jaded, and by now he and Longarm were starting to feel nervous with one another. So when he got Bonnie and her remaining gear to her stable in town with the help of the Indian police they cut a new deal. He said since she had really lost a horse to halve her profit from the deposits left by the two dead gunslicks, he would wire Uncle Sam to pay her for the one he had shot out from under her, even if it hadn't been anything like a forty-dollar horse. So she let him swap his own saddle and possibles to a fresh chestnut mare she said was steady and told him that he'd find it saddled and ready there whenever he wanted to ride.

He told Rain Crow he had some other errands to run now that he was in town. The Indians said they would wait for him at the all-night saloon near the depot. Longarm didn't see fit to remind them of the federal regulations regarding drunken Indians. If they could get served, dressed white, it wasn't his fight.

He went to the nearby Western Union office to wire Billy Vail about what he'd been up to so far and tell the boss he owed Bonnie Murphy forty bucks. It didn't take long, since in truth Longarm didn't have much to report that Vail hadn't already told him. He'd hoped perhaps a wire might be waiting for him about the identity of that spanking-new cowhand he'd had to gun in Denver, but old Billy never wasted the taxpayers' money on wires unless he had something to say, so Longarm knew that no news meant nothing new.

He went back outside. The town of Switchback wasn't

much when the sun was shining and was even less interesting at night unless a man aimed to get drunk or hire a whore. Longarm didn't feel up to either. He strode down to the saloon and peered in through the grimy window. Sure enough, the reservation police force was bellied up to the bar, drinking just like anybody else in the joint. He didn't want to cut their visit short, knowing the redeye they were getting in there had to be safer on their livers than the awful stuff they made themselves out on the reservation, so he ambled on to kill some time. It was a pleasant enough night and the moon made walking easy even where some fool had gunned a street lamp.

He didn't have a clear notion where he was headed until he spied the church steeple against the starry sky ahead. Then he knew where his wayward boots were carrying him, and he wondered if he really wanted to go.

He'd passed through these parts once before since the time old Roping Sally had been murdered by those land grabbers. The last time had been broad daylight, and he'd seen to it there were fresh-picked flowers in the mason jar on Sally's grave in the old churchyard. It had been depressing enough by daylight. What was the sense of visiting an old, dead love at this infernal hour?

The boardwalk ended. The path ahead was weedy and horse-turded. He knew the path on the far side of the dirt road was wider and firmer-packed, so he crossed over. Then he stopped by a board fence and lit a smoke as he wondered, once more, why.

He shook out the match, shrugged, and headed on to see how Sally was doing tonight. He didn't see how it could do her any good, but it couldn't hurt her. Nothing could hurt her now, and it wasn't like he had better places to go.

He swung a corner and walked under the dark archway formed by some sad old willow trees as, somewhere in the night, an owlbird hooted. He grimaced and muttered, "I ain't an Indian, owl. I know when I'm walking in the valley of the shadow, because *we* got sense enough to write on tombstones, not listen for medicine signs. But if you're Roping Sally's fourth spirit . . . howdy, Sally. I ain't afraid of any of your spirits, you pretty little thing."

It was funny how some Indians said everyone had four spirits. White folk had enough trouble believing they had one. But, according to the Dream Singers, when someone died, their spirit, soul, or whatever split into four parts, four being a medicine number as confusing as the white man's Trinity. They said it didn't matter whether you'd been good or bad to *two* of your spirits. One flew off to live forever in the lodge of Old Woman, whose lodge fire made the northern lights in the northern sky. Another of your four spirits got to do just about anything it liked in the Happy Hunting Ground, where no hunter ever missed, it never got too hot or cold or dry or wet, and all the women were pretty and willing. But two of your spirits had to stay behind: one to watch over your kin and guide them with dreams and other omens, while your fourth spirit, or ghost, either wandered aimlessly or scared people, depending on what sort of person you'd been. That was probably the spirit the Cheyenne were worried about when they cut off a fallen foe's bow fingers so his ghost couldn't shoot ghost arrows at them in revenge.

"Jesus!" he muttered aloud, stopping in his tracks in the considerable gloom as he told himself to snap out of it. There was no reason for him to be feeling so spooked, at least a city block from the nearest graveyard. But, for some reason, he was. He didn't know why, but the hairs on his neck were tingling enough for a kid exploring a haunted house at midnight.

That was something to study on. Longarm didn't believe

in haunts and, even if he had, the only dead person he knew in these parts was a good old gal who'd kissed him sweet and sassy the last time they'd met up. He couldn't be afraid of an old dead girl friend. It was something else that was tingling him.

He turned around. There was nothing following him. But he noticed his back didn't tingle as much when it was aimed at the churchyard, where a gal he trusted lay buried.

He was about to call himself a nervous Nelly, afraid of the dark, when he heard a soft, sneaky crunch somewhere between him and the lit-up parts of Switchback. So he eased open a nearby wooden gate set in an arch of rambler roses and backed into someone's front yard, drawing his .44.

A million years later, when most would have decided they'd been hearing bumps in the night, Longarm heard a voice whisper, "Cover me. I'm going around."

Longarm waited grimly, covering the path from the darkness of the yard. Then, just as a dark figure slunk into view and Longarm was about to take someone alive for a damned change, a door opened behind him, outlining him as it spilled lamplight all the way to the middle of the street. A quavering old she-male voice called out, "Who's there? Who's there? Oh, Lord, there *is* someone in my yard! Get him, Spot!"

All hell broke loose as the now illuminated man on the path drew on Longarm's black outline, Longarm threw down on him, and a small bundle of heroic fluff tore into Longarm's legs from the rear.

The pissy little dog didn't really get all his pissy little teeth through Longarm's stovepipe boot. But Longarm found it mighty distracting to gunfight in lousy light with an infernal dog hanging on his infernal right leg, growling like a runaway coffee grinder, while a hysterical old woman beat him on the head with a broom.

He didn't give a damn about her dog. Anything that ornery deserved anything it got. But the scared old lady was in the right as well as a human being, so Longarm had no choice but to end the confusion by shooting serious before anyone on *his* side of the fence could get hurt. The gunshots scared the poor old woman into running back inside and slamming her front door, wailing that she was being killed. Longarm kicked the dog loose, kicked it again to send it under the house, and eased out to see who'd *really* been killed this time.

He had only nailed one, the one who'd drawn on him. The one covering from around the corner hadn't been hit by the shots Longarm had pegged blind that way through the willow leaves for luck. He'd run off before his luck ran out.

Even in a town as rough as Switchback, that much gunplay was bound to arouse some curiosity. So by the time Longarm had lifted another wallet belonging to a Mr. Smith and was reloading his weapon, a lot of Switchback was running his way. A familiar voice called out his name and Longarm yelled back, "Over here, Rain Crow. Watch where you step, rounding the corner."

The Indian stared soberly down at the dead white man. "Heya, you have had a busy night, even for you, Longarm. Who was he?" he asked.

"Said his name was Smith. Could have been fibbing. Did you notice anyone running the other way just now? I got one son of a bitch left over."

Rain Crow said he hadn't as the crowd got thicker. A louder voice called out, "What in the hell's going on here?" Then Sheriff Murphy spotted Longarm, gun still in hand, and said, "Oh, I heard you were back, Longarm. What do you do, send away for these poor bastards? Who'd you gun this time?"

"I was hoping you or someone here in town might be able to tell me, Murph," Longarm said. "I know for a fact two of his pals hired mounts off your niece, Miss Bonnie. So the gang must have been in town longer than me."

Sheriff Murphy, a tough old gent not half as pretty as his niece, gasped. "Jesus, is Bonnie all right? I just come from my own place, and—"

"Bonnie's safe and well. We can talk about her later," Longarm cut in. "Right now I want to talk about this son of a bitch at my feet. Has anyone here ever seen him before?"

A townee in shirtsleeves and a dark canvas apron volunteered, "I have. He and three other gents was drinking at my place just this afternoon. I run the Pronghorn, over by the depot. Ain't seen any of 'em this evening."

Longarm said, "I ain't surprised, and I'm much obliged. That means I still got one to worry about. But the odds are sure starting to even out."

Murphy sighed. "You call them odds even, Longarm? Afore I'd go up against you lonesome, I'd just swallow my pride and do some running!"

Longarm nodded. "Rain Crow, you know where Miss Bonnie's livery is. Get there on the double and make sure none of her horses get rid without my approval. Murphy, I'm counting on you to cover the depot, so get to it."

Murphy started to point out that he was an elected public official, not Longarm's valet. But he was a good lawman himself, and there were times to argue rank and times to just get at it. So he got at it, calling out to a couple of his deputies in the crowd to follow him as he headed for the depot.

Rain Crow and his own boys were, of course, already gone by then, so Longarm faced the still considerable crowd and said, "All right, who wants to be a federal deputy? The pay's a dollar a day and a free funeral if you fuck up."

95

Nobody answered, so he pointed at a couple of healthy-looking cowhands. "You and you. I want this way out of town bottled up. You can give me your names later. You, there, in the derby hat. You look bigger than the one who got away. Get some of your pals together and cover the south road out of town. I can't see him running on to the Indian reserve to the west, and there's nothing to the east a man afoot could get to this side of sunrise. What are you all waiting for, a kiss goodbye?"

Everyone laughed and the crowd started to thin as others learned how much fun it was to hunt in their own back yards. Longarm stopped the barkeep of the Pronghorn. "Hold it. I need some more help from you. I know where to find the undertaker and the coroner from my last stop here, but I want you to tell me if those mysterious strangers could have arrived by way of the noon train from the south or the three o'clock train from the north."

The barkeep thought for a moment. "They was in my place before three. Is that any help?"

"It is. It narrows it down to getting here ahead of me from the south or being here waiting at least overnight. I'll study on the overnight angle later. Right now I want you to think back and tell me if you can remember anything outstanding about any of 'em. Anyone can be a Smith or Jones, and I know none of 'em are famous enough in the States to have made the Wanted posters I read regular."

The barkeep shrugged and said, "They was just regular-looking gents, dressed cow. I mean, I never noticed no tattoos or peg legs, if that's what you mean."

"I know what at least three of them looked like, and the fourth's a stranger here in town, who'll stand out no matter what he looks like. I want you to think before you answer. Did they talk about anything you might recall, now that you know they were owlhoots?"

96

The barkeep thought, but shook his head sadly. "They was just bellied up to the bar long enough to wet their whistles. Wait... one of 'em came in later, then all four left. So the first three was likely waiting for him, right?"

"You're doing fine. Could you narrow the time down better?"

"Not hardly. They wasn't causing any trouble and I had rougher trade to deal with. You know how some young cowhands act with a couple of beers in 'em. Oh, hold it. I just remembered. The one who come in to tell the others something must have done so just after the afternoon train arrived. I recalls it now because a whiskey drummer I know come in to sell me some liquor just as they were leaving, and he did say he'd just arrived on the afternoon train from the south. Does that help you any, Deputy?"

"It does," said Longarm. "It adds up just as I suspicioned. They were laying for me here ahead of time. When I failed to show, two rode out to catch me down the line. When one's hired mount come back alone, the two left went to see why and hid the results. Now if only I could prove they were Canadians. Do you recall if they had Canadian accents?"

"I don't know. I never noticed Canadians talking all that different from normal folk, Deputy."

"Most Americans don't, and we and they sound just the same to folk in England, I've been told. They only say a few words like 'out' and 'house' a mite different from us, and all of 'em don't even do that. You'd have noticed *French* Canadian accents, wouldn't you?"

"Oh, sure, we get a few of them in here now and again, this close to the border. Trader out to the Blackfoot reserve's a French Canuck. He talks amusing as hell. But that wasn't the way them four cowhands talked. They was just the same as you and me. I wouldn't have recalled as much about 'em

97

as I just did, had you not nudged my brain so. How do you do that, anyway? I had no notion I was so smart till you started asking me about them rascals."

Longarm shrugged and said, "Asking the right questions just takes a little practice. I've been at it six or eight years."

Some new faces were appearing in the crowd now. Longarm recognized the local undertaker from his last visit. "Sheriff Murphy says you has another customer for me here, Longarm," the man said. He looked down, whistled, and added, "Murphy always has been a truthful cuss. Who do we send the bill to on this one?"

"I'm still working on that, Doc. Meanwhile, could you at least get him off the street for now?"

The friendly undertaker said he could. Longarm plucked a rose from over the gate they were standing in front of and said he was going off to study some, alone, on his next move.

He walked on to the churchyard. He had no trouble finding Sally's marker, since he'd paid for it. He removed his hat, alone in the moonlight, and gently placed the single rose on the dead girl's grave. Then he said, "I don't know which of your four spirits was looking out for me tonight, Roping Sally. But I thank it, anyway. All four of you are ever thoughtful."

Chapter 9

The night clerk at the Western Union office couldn't recall anyone in a new white Stetson either sending or receiving wires in the past few nights, but he added that he couldn't swear to what the other shifts had been up to. Longarm asked him to haul out the log books. When the clerk protested that Longarm had no notion how many wires he could be talking about, the tall deputy smiled down at him and replied, "You don't have to read me every word sent or received by folk you know personal. How many wires could strangers have gotten or sent in a town where strangers bring the women to the windows?"

"I'm not supposed to discuss company business with outsiders, Deputy Long."

"You ain't. You just now *called* me a *deputy*. Make that U. S. federal deputy and let's cut the bullshit. I go through this all the time with you spark wranglers and, so far, Western Union ain't won yet. So the sooner you get cracking, the sooner I'll be leaving you to your dime novel or whatever. I ain't leaving till you do."

The night clerk muttered a lot but, after leafing through a mess of carbon flimsies, he finally managed to come up with one wire from Denver, sent here to a John J. Smith, informing him his Aunt Lulu would be arriving in Switchback aboard the afternoon train and suggesting she'd been led to expect a warm welcome from her darling nephews.

The message had been signed, "Uncle John." Longarm grimaced and growled, "For such a humorous bunch, they sure are uninventive when it comes to names. Of course, if I was trying to make up French names, off the cuff, I can hardly think of any unusual ones. Yeah, a French-talking lawman might find Duval or Cartier sort of common, too."

He lit a cheroot thoughtfully, then asked the night clerk, "Quick, without thinking, make me up a German name!"

"Uh . . . Schultz?"

"Good enough. It makes my point. Now all I got to do is figure out whether I'm being smart as hell or playing chess when the name of the game is checkers. Some of our home-grown owlhoots can act dumb as hell too, so I'd best catch one of the bastards and find out how good his English is."

He took a drag on the cheroot, let it out, and asked, "If I was a poor wayfaring stranger here in Switchback, where would I find a not-too-fussy place to stay? I mean a place as don't ask questions or keep records as to who may or may not have been on the premises recent?"

The night clerk shrugged. "Don't look at me. I'm a married man and my wife's bigger than me. I've heard tell of shady ladies on the wrong side of the stockyards as well as tracks. But I don't know if you can rent them by the hour or the night. They'd know at the all-night saloon, I reckon."

Longarm said he was much obliged and left. He didn't go to the saloon to ask where the small town's modest tenderloin was. Any man who'd ever herded cows in his misspent youth knew how to find a whorehouse if a whorehouse was to be found.

There was a block of them, as the night clerk had suggested, downwind of the railside loading pens and municipal dump. He could hear the pianos and see the pathetic fancy gals lounging under the red lanterns over the crib doors as he strode the narrow cinder-paved lane between them.

100

An anxious, ugly old gal who looked either Mexican or Digger Indian broke the rules by stepping clean away from the shanty she'd been holding up with her half-bare back and grabbing Longarm by his left elbow, smiling up at him like a begging dog used to getting kicked as often as fed, and said, *"Buenoches, vaquero. 'Onde va?"*

Longarm kept his feeling to himself as he replied, "With you, if you've got a minute."

She looked like an orphan who'd just spied Santa Claus no matter what the other kids said. She dragged him inside as, outside, another she-male voice protested loudly, "You'll be sorry, cowboy! That greaser bitch has crabs as well as the pox!"

The whore who'd snared him slammed her door shut triumphantly, saying, "Do not listen to that jealous bitch, *querido*. I am far famed for my health as well as passion!"

Longarm said he was sure she was as he took in the interior of her hovel. There wasn't much to take in. A saggy mattress on boxes covered with a filthy sheet took up most of the one room. Such sanitary facilities as there were consisted of a couple of damp gray towels on hooks near the foot of her sordid bed and a wash-bowl in a corner. It smelled like the water needed changing, despite the incense sticks she'd been burning since her last customer. There was no place fit to sit in even a trail-soiled suit. So he remained standing as she shucked her one-piece cotton shift and got on the bed, saying, "I am beautiful, no? I do not wish for to sound unromantic, but my admirers usually give me a present."

Longarm took out his wallet and said, "That sounds fair. What do you generally charge?"

"Ah, two dollars, *querido*?"

"I'm giving you five, for I'm asking something special tonight." The whore reached up to take the sawbuck, but eyed him waringly. "I hope you are not interested in pain! Forgive me, I mean no disrespect, and you are *muy* good-looking, but even gentle love-making with a man as big as you could fatigue a woman as small as me!"

"I wouldn't want to do that," Longarm said. "So I ain't paying you for your usual services. I'm the law."

"Oh, no! It is not just!" she sobbed, sitting up and grabbing for her duds. "You cannot arrest me! We have done nothing! I only invited you in for to shelter you from the rain and it was you who insisted I take my clothes off!"

He laughed. "Simmer down. I ain't *that* kind of law. I only want to ask you a few questions."

"What kind of questions? I know nothing. If I knew something, I would not tell you. Do you think I wish to spend the rest of my life with the mark of the *vaca* carved in my face?"

"I ain't asking about any of the other gals, or their pimps, either. I know you've paid your dues to the local political machine and I ain't out to arrest them either. What the voters of a town decide to do about local country matters ain't federal. But if you ain't willing to talk about nobody, you'd best give back the money and we'll say no more about it. I'm sure there's others who'll be more willing at the going rates for street informants."

She clutched the money as well as her shift to her bare breasts possessively as she asked, "What is it you wish for to know?"

He told her about the men who'd been laying for him and asked her what she knew about them, adding, "Don't make nothing up. I always find out when folk has lied to me, and I'll be testy as hell if you put a new white Stetson where it never was, just to earn your pay."

She sighed, held out the crumpled note, and said, "I have seen no such person in this part of town. I wish I had.

Business has been most slow since the spring roundup."

He smiled down at her pleasantly. *"Bueno.* I think you told me the truth. So the money's yourn, *señorita."*

"Es verdad? I am called Concepcion, and I knew the *momento* I saw you that you were a generous one. I needed this money, most *desperado,* as you must have guessed. But I feel strange keeping it, having done so little for it. Would you like for to use me as a woman, now?"

"Already have," he said. "I figured a woman would be more likely to have heard the gossip in these parts. I'd best get over to the other parts of town now. Those rascals must have been staying some infernal place in town of late."

As he put a hand on her latch, Concepcion stood up, letting her rags fall away to face him, stark, with all her charms exposed. They might have tempted him more had she been a mite younger. He just smiled nicely, said he'd keep her kind offer in mind, and got out of there.

Rain Crow and the other Indian police were waiting for Longarm at the saloon. They didn't seem too drunk, but he knew they weren't fixing to get cold sober in such surroundings, so he told them they could head back to the reserve now. When Rain Crow asked if he didn't need an escort back himself, Longarm said, "Ain't sure I'm going this side of sunrise. A lady I just talked to said it looked like rain and, meanwhile, there's a hunter's moon tonight. I'm just going to poke about here in Switchback till I either catch that last son of a bitch or make sure he's left town. Got some more wires to send, too, as soon as I have more questions to ask."

Rain Drow frowned. "There is a telegraph set out at the agency, and Crimmins can send anything you like to anywhere, Longarm."

The tall deputy shrugged. "I've been known to tap a key

or two in my own time, too. Learned how in the army. But it's getting late, and I don't aim to disturb the agent and his wife. If they ask about me, tell 'em I'll likely get out there again sometime tomorrow."

"But, Longarm, don't you want to see if we can cut the trail of those Cree as soon as it's light? I thought you were sent to help us, not to poke about here in *town!*"

Longarm said, "You and your young men hunt for sign on the prairie if you like. If them raiders was leaving clear trails to anywhere important, there'd be no point to this investigation. I said I'd be back out there when I had a reason to be back out there, Rain Crow. Do I have to say it again?"

The Indian shrugged, muttered to his sidekicks in Blackfoot, and they all filed out, leaving Longarm at the bar, but not alone. A burly gent dressed cow laughed and said, "That's putting the sassy redskins in their place, pard!"

Longarm didn't want to be his pard. He picked up his schooner of needled beer and moved over to a corner table. The man he had snubbed looked thoughtfully at him. But then the barkeep leaned over to him and murmured something, so he turned around to quit while he was ahead. Longarm made a mental note that folk were gossiping about him in Switchback, too. But it couldn't be helped, given the size of the little jerkwater town.

Someone else must have been talking about him being in town, too, for a few minutes later a gray-haired gent in army blue came through the batwing doors, glanced around, and came directly to Longarm's table. He sat down and introduced himself as a Captain Gatewood, from nearby Fort Banyon. Longarm saw no reason to disbelieve him. Gatewood wore railroad tracks on his shoulders and lots of officers were growing overage in grade, thanks to President Hayes, who didn't drink and apparently thought the peacetime army could get along mighty frugal, too.

Captain Gatewood must not have agreed with the First Lady, Lemonade Lucy Hayes. For when a waitress gal in a shocking flamenco skirt came over, she brought him a shot glass and bottle of Kentucky, unasked. The officer started to tell her to bring another shot glass for Longarm, but Longarm said he only drank Maryland rye when he wasn't on duty and asked what else he could do for the army.

"We heard you were coming," Gatewood said. "You're on record as a damned good army scout, too. I'm taking my troop out after Cree in the morning. Are you interested?"

Longarm took a sip of needled beer before he said, "Ain't sure. Have you really cut their trail, or are you just patroling, Captain?"

Gatewood frowned and asked, "Now how in the hell are we to catch the red rascals if we don't patrol for sign, Longarm?"

"Don't get your bowels in an uproar," Longarm said. "I've got even better reasons for wanting at least one war party rounded up. They damn near turned me bald-headed just this evening."

That naturally interested the army man, so Longarm went on to bring Gatewood up to date on his own active career of late. When he'd finished, the captain said, "Hot damn! You say it was on the wagon trace betwixt here and the Blackfoot agency? That's where me and my boys will start looking in the morning, then."

Longarm said, "Make sure they don't get excited when they see other Indians, then. I know this may not be any business of mine, but ain't you supposed to get permission from the B.I.A. afore you lead any cavalry charges through a reserve of Friendlies?"

Gatewood helped himself to a healthy slug of Kentucky

and said, "You're right. It's none of your business. But I'll tell you anyway. For once War and Interior are in total agreement on Indian policy. We have permission from the B.I.A. They had to give it to us. The Blackfoot reserve runs smack up to the border between Canada and these United States, and if there's one thing nobody can argue about, it's the right and, hell, duty of the U. S. Army to secure the borders of these United States against all comers, red, white, or purple!"

Longarm chuckled. "I've heard that somewhere," he admitted. "They keep jawing about a separate regular border patrol, under Immigration. But unless old Hayes finds more money, which he ain't about to in an election year, you boys have your job cut out for you. There's . . . what? . . . eighty miles of border between the Blackfoot reserve and Canada alone?"

Gatewood swallowed another belt. "Closer to ninety," he said. "It's obvious enough why those Cree have chosen that route into our land of the free. Anywhere else, they might stand out more. But all Indians look alike to us real Americans, so—"

Longarm blinked in surprise and cut in to protest, "Jesus! You can't tell a *Blackfoot* from a *Cree* when you see one? Leaving out who the real Americans might be, the Blackfoot are called Blackfeet because they all wear blue moccasins, which Cree don't. Another sure sign of a Blackfoot is that U-shaped decoration they fancy. Whether it's beadwork or painted, they look like somebody typed a long line of upper case U's across their shirt fringe, shield rim, or whatever. Oh, yeah, Plains Cree wear more feathers. Blackfoot like dingle-dangle strips of white weasel fur where most High Plains Indians would stick feathers. Should you see a gent coming at you in a regular war bonnet in the near future, he'll likely be a Cree. The Lakota have been quiet this

106

summer. If an Indian's wearing what looks more like a floor mop, he's more likely on our side."

Gatewood took yet another drink, stared sort of owlishly at Longarm and asked, "How come Blackfoot are called Blackfoot if they got *blue* feet?"

Longarm chuckled. "Mistranslation. The so-called Black Hills got their name the same way. Early travelers asked the Lakota, or what you may call Sioux, the names of things in these parts. The Lakota tongue is sort of vague about the colors black and blue."

"You mean the Sioux are color-blind?"

"Not hardly. Translating *Nadene* to English gets into the same fix with *blue* and *green*. One professor wrote quite a paper on what he called inbred color-blindness amongst Navajo school kids one time. It upset the B.I.A. so much they tested a bunch of the kids' eyes. And guess what? A Nadene speaker can pick out blue from green as good as you or me. They just happen to consider them two shades of one color in their own lingo. The Lakota have different words for blue and green. But they consider *black* a dark shade of *blue,* see?"

"No, I don't see! Anyone who lacks names for two different colors entire must be ignorant as hell."

Longarm took off his tobacco-brown Stetson and placed it on the mahogany table between them, asking, "What color is my hat, Captain?"

Gatewood said, "Dark brown, of course. Are you trying to say I'm drunk?"

"Don't have to. What color is this table?"

Gatewood scowled down, suddenly grinned knowingly, and said, "I see the way you mean to trick me. But it won't work. Anyone can see we're talking about two *shades* of brown!"

Longarm nodded, held out one of his suntanned wrists,

and said, "Here's another. You couldn't hardly call my hide pink or lavender. But when you study on it, these three browns, here, could be called three entire different colors, if we wasn't agreed the only name we have to work with is brown. We say coffee brown, chocolate brown, leaf brown, and such, for what are really dozens of different colors when you study on it. So who are we to say an Indian don't have the right to call the color of grass and the color of the sky two shades of the same color, or black not a dark shade of blue? The trouble don't come up with the Blackfoot themselves, by the way. They *have* different words for blue and black. But they call themselves Piegan, not Blackfoot, anyways, and—"

"Damn it, Longarm, are you trying to confuse me?" the captain interrupted.

"I reckon it would be needless effort, Captain. I'm sure reassured to see a man who knows Indians so good is riding through Indian country in the morning. By the way, I know Lemonade Lucy's an old fuss, but do you really aim to mount up with that whole bottle under your belt?"

Gatewood dispensed with the shot glass this time, sucking his bottle like a gray-headed baby before he growled, "Shit, my horse doesn't stagger no matter how much I drink, and you're right about that old fool, Lemonade Lucy Hayes."

"You're talking about the First Lady, Captain."

"Bull. The first lady was Mother Eve. It says so in the Good Book. Hey, you're not a Cat-Licker, are you?"

Longarm could see Gatewood was getting to that stage where his mind was starting to grasshopper. But to humor the fool until his head hit the table Longarm shook his own head and said, "Not hardly. Licking cats sounds sort of disgustful."

Gatewood nodded judiciously and said, "Damned right. I don't hold with Popery, neither. It's them French Canadian Cat-Lickers' fault we got to go hunt Canadian Indians in the cussed cruel cold dawn. If it was up to me we'd send 'em all back where they come from. I don't see why we had to let the damned Indians in the country in the first place."

Longarm didn't answer. He'd finished his one beer schooner in the time it had taken the cavalryman to get falling down drunk. Getting a refill could make for a graceful rise from this particular table. So Longarm murmured something about beer and scraped his chair back. Gatewood blinked his eyes to focus them and growled, "Siddown, boy. I ain't through talking to you. Are you with me or against me?"

"About what?" asked Longarm wearily.

Gatewood said, "Them Roman Cat-Lickers, of course. If that half-breed, Louis Riel, wasn't stirring up the Cat-Licker Injuns with his bloody banner, I'd get to sleep late in the morning."

Gatewood wasn't what one could call wide awake right now. But Longarm had learned about wisdom from the lips of babes and drunken fools in his time. He nodded soberly. "Tell me some more about this bloody banner of yourn, Captain."

Gatewood said, "Shit, it ain't *my* bloody banner. It's the battle flag of the Metis Separatist Movement. Riel and the other Red River Breeds sets store in being Injun as well as French-talking Roman Cat-Lickers. I'll be hanged if I see why. I'd be ashamed to be either."

"Could we stick to the business about a bloody banner? I've got a reason for asking."

Gatewood took another swig of liquor and said, "Riel's battle flag is homemade from a cotton sheet stamped or painted with a mess of them fancy French floors-to-lay."

"Do you mean fleurs-de-lis?"

"Yeah, them fancy floors they had on the old Frog flag, before the revolution. Only the old kings had gold whatevers on a field of white. Those halfbreed French Canucks have the floors-to-lay red on white. They say the red is oxblood and that the bloody banner stands for Frogs who are both red and white. I suspect the Pope put 'em up to it."

Longarm didn't answer. He'd been assured by others just as certain that it was either the Jews or the Freemasons stirring up Indian trouble on the sly. So Gatewood put his head down on the mahogany by the bottle and Longarm tried not to disturb him as he eased to his feet and away, beer schooner in hand. He moved over to the bar with it, but before he could get a refill one of Sheriff Murphy's deputies tore in, out of breath, to gasp, "Longarm, the sheriff was hoping you'd still be in town. He sent me looking for you."

"You found me. What's up, pard?"

"We got him. That last white hat you said might still be in town. He was boarding with a dumb old widow woman on the edge of town. But she wasn't that dumb, and—"

"Never mind how you found out where he was staying," Longarm cut in, "just lead me to where you're holding the son of a bitch. I got questions to ask that old boy!"

"Come with me and I'll carry you to the sheriff and the others, then, the deputy replied. "But I fear that owlhoot's answering days are over."

As they left together Longarm sighed and said, "Damn, I thought I heard distant gunshots a spell back. I put it down to some lonesome cowhand baying at the moon. Couldn't you boys take him alive?"

"Sure we could have, if he'd acted sensible. Sheriff Murphy gave him a chance to throw out his guns and come out peaceable. But the rascal yelled back that we'd never take him alive and, you know what, he was right!"

Chapter 10

There were no street lamps on the side street where the boarding house stood. But enough gents were waving torches for Longarm to make out an old lady bawling on the porch steps as two neighbor ladies comforted her. A skinny kid wearing a copper badge and a twelve-gauge shotgun was standing guard in the doorway, but he stood aside for Longarm and his guide as they went in.

Sheriff Murphy, other lawmen, and a gent Longarm recalled from his last visit as the country coroner were lounging about the front parlor. Murphy was seated on the horsehair sofa, looking sort of pleased with himself, with the body spread on the rug at his feet like a hunting trophy. The rug was never going to be the same, no matter how much the old woman outside beat it.

Someone had rolled the dead man face up, but Longarm didn't recognize what the number nine buck and busted glass had left of the face. Murphy said laconically, "Never peer out a window after calling a Murphy a cocksucker unless you're sure Murphy's left his shotgun home. His wallet says his name was Bob White. Ain't that a bitch?"

Longarm grimaced and replied, "That's an improvement on Smith, but I somehow doubt his wallet's word. I'll put a description of him on the wire, but an average-sized white man with no distinguishing features ain't likely to make interesting reading."

The coroner said, "This one's not as boring as the one you bored at the far end of town this evening, Longarm. Take a closer look at his left hand."

111

Longarm dropped to one knee, raised the cadaver's limp left wrist to the coal-oil light, and saw a small blue star tattooed on the web of the thumb. He nodded. "Yeah, that's the sort of kid stuff convicts do to themselves with a needle and burnt cork to kill the time."

He unbuttoned the cuffs of both wrists and pushed up the sleeves. As everyone saw the more professional red-and-blue anchor design tattooed on the dead man's right forearm, Murphy whistled and asked, "How did you know about that, Longarm?"

Longarm unbuttoned the cadaver's shirt as he replied, "Mankind can be divided into those who fancy tattoos and those who don't. It's dumb as hell for an outlaw to wear even one tattoo, but I've noticed the things tend to come in bunches. This old boy seems to have been a sailor at some time or another, so..."

They all whistled as one when they saw the full rigged man-of-war sailing across the dead man's exposed bare chest. Murphy leaned forward for a better look, pointed at the battle flag waving across pale dead flesh from the yardarm of the impressive vessel, and said, "Hot damn! That must be a pirate ship. Look at that black flag, Longarm!"

Longarm nodded soberly and said, "Yeah, that was done convict style with carbon black, too. At some time and for some reason this old boy wanted the ship's original colors inked out." He glanced up at the coroner and asked, "Is there any way to restore this blacked-out banner, Doc?"

"Do I look like a tattoo artist, Longarm? I'm paid to determine the cause of death, not turn back the clock. All that tattoo ink's been under that dead hide quite a spell, judging from the way it's faded. Undertaker might know more about such matters. He's more skilled at corpse cosmetics. He should be here any minute."

Longarm rose and consulted his watch. "I'll talk to him

112

later. It's late as hell and I figure to wake some lawmen as it is. I got to send a mess of wires."

As he started to leave, the sheriff asked him where he would be if they needed him later that night. Longarm replied that the night was nearly over and that he had no notion where he meant to spend the rest of it, but that he'd check back with Murphy before he left for the Blackfoot Agency or went anywhere else important.

At the Western Union he had to bang hard on the counter a few times before the same clerk came out from the back, rubbing his eyes. Longarm said he was sorry as hell he had to distract him from his duties, but that they had a mess of messages to get off, adding, "Most of 'em can go night letter rates, since it ain't polite to ring doorbells after midnight, but the important ones go straight. So let's get cracking."

He took command of a stub pencil and a pad of telegram blanks and printed almost as neat and fast as old Henry back at the office could manage with a typewriter. As he finished one he would tear it off and hand it to the clerk before starting the next, as methodically as a machine. The clerk said he sure could fill out forms fast. Longarm said, "Don't you dare tell my office. I hate paperwork. Why are you standing there staring at me like an owl bird, old son? I want these messages to go *out* tonight, hear?"

The clerk muttered that it was already more like morning and headed back to his telegraph desk with the first sheaf of yellow blanks.

Longarm had just finished his query to the Navy Department, night letter, when the clerk came back to the counter to say, "I can't send this message to Fort MacLeod."

"Sure you can," Longarm said. "It's just across the border, up Alberta way, and Crown Sergeant Foster of the Mounties never goes to sleep this early. Sometimes I suspicion that muley redcoat never sleeps at all. We've had our differences in the past, but he's a good old boy, and if there's anyone who'd know about Canadian rebel flags—"

"The wire's down," the clerk cut in. "This is the second or third time this summer that someone's cut our wire to Canada. Must have been cut on the far side of the border, since our repair crews can't locate the break south of it."

Longarm frowned thoughtfully and asked, "How long's it been out?"

The western Union man said, "Three or four days. Must have been cut by the Metis or their Indian allies. There's nothing we can do until the Canadians do something about it north of the border, see?"

Longarm shook his head. "Nope. I don't see. Fort MacLeod ain't far from the border. That's why the Mounties built her there in the first damn place. So how come they ain't been able to find the break and splice it in all this time?"

"Maybe they've been wiped out, like Custer?" the clerk suggested, cheerfully enough, considering.

It was something to think about, so Longarm did. Then he shook his head. "This may not sound too patriotic, but had Mounties rode against the Lakota Confederacy that time on the Little Bighorn, I'd have put my money on the Mounties. I've been to Fort MacLeod. Foster and his troops are forted good. I met old Louis Riel in the flesh not too long ago, too. He struck me as a sensible gent. Too sensible to attack a fortified British outpost with his ragged-ass so-called rebel army."

The clerk shrugged and said, "Oh, I don't know, they say Riel's rebellion has heated up considerable in the last few weeks. He's got that mule-headed MacDonald administration and their infernal Creeping and Paralysis Railroad really worried, now that poor whites as well as full-blood Indians have started to rally to his Metis flag. Maybe your Mountie pals at Ford MacLeod are afraid to come out from their walls even to look for the break in the wire."

"You don't know Crown Sergeant Foster," Longarm said. "First time we met he was willing to fight *me* and, in all modesty, I pack almost as much weaponry as all them poor Metis together."

"Oh, come on, Longarm. The papers say Louis Riel has gathered hundreds and hundreds of angry breeds, full bloods, and poor whites!"

"Maybe. But all they are, without training, is a mob. Without modern weapons, they're even less. I told you I've met folk from both sides. Riel's boys may or may not be in the right, but few of 'em even have a repeating rifle to call their own, while at Ford MacLeod, the government keeps gatlings and field artillery in addition to disciplined, well-armed mounted police. Last I heard, Canada had its own *army*, too, if push ever really comes to shove up there."

He thought, then sighed and said, "Well, whatever's going on, I can't wire Foster right now. So keep the form and send it when you can. I'll get back in a spell to pick up any answers."

Outside, the street lamps had all burned out by now and the moon was fixing to set. That left at least two hours of mighty dark between here and the first day glow from the east. The mount waiting for him at Bonnie's livery wouldn't know the trail to the Indian agency, and he wouldn't be much help if he couldn't see it. But if he couldn't see the prairie all about as they crossed it, nobody else out there could see them, so what the hell.

He went first to the sheriff's office. The sleepy deputy on duty said Murphy had gone home to bed. Longarm knew the local law wasn't desperate to see him at the moment.

115

He left a message he was headed back to the agency and that there was a telegraph wire handy if anything came up before he got back to town. Then he went to the undertaker's, or, in Switchback's case, the place where the part-time undertaker did business. The storefront was dark. He guessed undertakers slept once in a while, too. So he left a note under the door, asking them not to bury the latest rascal until they saw if there was any way to find out what sort of a battle flag he'd blacked out on his chest.

Then he went to get his hired chestnut, wondering what he'd do if the livery was locked up for the night as well.

It wasn't. The big sliding door was open a dark slit, for nobody but a fool left a lantern burning in a straw-filled building untended. He slid it open, called out, "Anybody here?" and, when nobody but a nickering pony answered him, struck a match. He found a lamp and lit it. He found the chestnut waiting in a front stall, but Bonnie had left the bridle and saddle over the rail with a fresh saddle blanket handy. He nodded and said, "Good. You feel up to some night riding, old gal?"

The mare didn't answer. Bonnie did. She came out from the back, holding a candlestick in one hand and the front of her robe closed with the other. Her red hair was unpinned and hung down over her breasts, which was just as well when one considered how thin her white cotton robe was.

"Howdy, Red," Longarm said. "I'm sorry I woke you."

"You didn't," she told him. "I haven't been able to get to sleep. Right now I'm a bundle of nerves. Do you have to leave right now? It feels like three in the morning."

"You're close enough. What's got you so upset you can't sleep, Red?"

She laughed wearily and said, "Listen to him, Lord. He almost gets me scalped. Then he runs all over town shooting people without a word of explanation to me, at least, and he wonders why I can't get to sleep. God damn it, Custis,

I want you to tell me what in the hell is going *on* around here!"

He said it was a long and tedious tale. She said, "Let's go back to my quarters, then, and I'll put the coffee on."

He snuffed the lamp to follow her by candlelight, observing, "I wouldn't drink more coffee if I was aiming to try to sleep now. You're already wound up tense, no offense."

"What would you suggest, then, Custis?"

"Well, most of them she-male tonics ladies is allowed to drink are about a hundred proof. That's likely why ladies find 'em so calming to their delicate nerves."

Bonnie laughed. "I've got some some plain old Bombay gin. I'm neither a lady nor a hypocrite. Why didn't I think of that myself?"

She led him into a crib not much larger but a lot nicer-smelling than the one Concepcion had in a less desirable neighborhood. She told him to make himself comfortable and, since there was no place to sit but her bouncy bedstead, that was where he wound up, sitting up like a gent on a sofa.

Bonnie ducked through a beaded curtain into the darkness of what had to be her kitchen and came back out with a square gin bottle and a couple of tumblers. She sat beside him and poured them both awesome drinks.

"I haven't had any of this for some time," she said. "It's funny how I seldom think to drink strong spirits alone. But you're right. This may be just the thing to put me to sleep."

As she handed him a nearly filled hotel tumbler of straight gin he laughed and said, "I couldn't put all this away, even with a chaser, and rise to my full height in the foreseeable future, Red! I suggested a nightcap, not a lethal dose."

She said, "Just sip it, then. I'm not up to going to the pump out back in my nightie."

He started to offer to fetch the water. But then, as she

snuggled closer, guzzling gin, he wondered why in thunder he'd want to do a fool thing like that.

He had to put his free arm around her back to keep them from falling across the mattress together even before they got drunk enough to excuse it. She didn't seem to mind. She must not have noticed how thin her cotton shift was and, what the hell, he couldn't feel anything unmentionable through it. Though she did seem to have a mole on her upper left arm, now that he studied with his fingertips. Her hair smelled teasing, too, as she sipped her own gin and asked him to tell her all about everything.

It took a spell, even keeping it simple. So Longarm was feeling the little he'd nursed bringing her up to date. Bonnie seemed to like the taste of gin more. Most women did. But when she'd drained enough to start giggling in the wrong places, Longarm firmly took her tumbler from her, put it next to his fuller one on the bed table, and said, "That's enough. I was talking to someone earlier tonight who started losing track just as the conversation was getting interesting, and—"

"Was she prettier than me?" Bonnie cut in.

He sighed and said, "That's what I mean. Where were we? Oh, right. I suspicion that diamond design on the home-grown Indian flags is an attempt at the old French fleur-de-lis. Plains Indians go in for what fancy art critics back East call Symbolic Simple Something, and when you squint at both designs they're more or less the same general shape, at least. Everybody knows some of the full bloods have thrown in with Louis Riel and his Metis. I wonder what makes the current Canadian government so popular. Old President Hayes would have to go some to get the white nesters, Indians, and everyone in between mad at him all at once."

Bonnie snuggled closer and sang, "Old MacDonald had a railroad, toot, toot, toot, tootoot."

Longarm laughed. "Yeah, the transcontinental railroad they've been pushing through up north has sort of pushed right-of-way grants into what lots of Canadians I've met call land grabbing. But that don't explain why Plains Cree have invaded our country waving Riel's bloody banner."

"Maybe they got lost?" she suggested.

"Not hardly" he said. "The Indians were riding this range long before we were, and I've yet to meet anyone along the border who doesn't know it's there. You can miss it by a mile or more, since it ain't fenced, and one grass stem looks much the same as any other. But those riders who come at us earlier tonight were way more than a day's ride south of the border."

He took off his hat since, from the way she was leaning into him, he wasn't likely to rise and leave for a spell. As he placed it on the table with the bottle and glasses, Bonnie asked why he didn't take his gun rig off as well, since it was digging into her hip.

He sighed and said, "Not hardly. Sheriff Murphy favors a cross-draw, too, and last time I looked he was your *uncle!* We'd best stick to less tempting bedtime stories, Red. I've been wondering if someone's trying to stir up trouble between that sullen MacDonald and President Hayes by staging fake Canadian Indian raids. But that won't work at all. If I was out to get the U. S. Cavalry riding against Canada, I'd have raiders in red coats raising red down here. Hostile Indians, if that's what they are, could only serve to make the Cav and the Mounties work *together.*"

"Maybe someone's trying to patch up the disagreement betwixt them and us. And where's my drink? I don't care how the Canadian and U.S. political hacks feel about each other this summer. I want to get *drunk* with you, durn it!"

He sighed. "I don't reckon we should, Miss Bonnie. I'd hate to leave you with the impression I was a sissy, but I'm trying not to act like a lunatic, even if it hurts."

"How come? Don't you want to get drunk and . . . oh, hell, sleep with me, you shy old thing?"

Longarm laughed incredulously and said, "It ain't polite to make fun of your elders, Red. You can't be that drunk, yet."

She giggled. "I never said I was. I said I wanted to get laid. I ain't been laid since poor Randal passed on, nearly a year ago."

"Hold on!" he said. "Are you hinting you could be a widow woman, or at least not a virgin with a sheriff for an uncle?"

She shook her head to clear it and muttered, "I was never married to my uncle. That would have been silly as well as sinful. I was married to Randal. That's how I wound up with his livery business when he died of lockjaw. I don't mind telling you it upset me a heap. For my poor Randal was a lovesome man, almost as big as you."

What she'd said put a new complexion entirely on the situation. But Longarm still hesitated, remembering how good Sheriff Murphy was with a shotgun and, since he who hesitates is lost, he lost the chance to take Bonnie up on her kind offer. She suddenly went limp in his arms and started snoring.

He sighed, laid her out on the bed like a pretty corpse, and drew the covers up over her lest she catch cold sleeping off her gin in such a thin and gaping gown. Then he got to his feet, put on his hat, and snuffed the candle. As he let himself out in total darkness he told the tingle in his pants, "I know, old pard, I'm never going to forgive myself for this, either. But there's things a decent cuss can do, and there's things he just can't, no matter how tempting."

120

Chapter 11

Longarm made it back to his quarters at the Indian agency without getting scalped, or even waking anybody up as far as he could tell. He must have hit the feathers tired, for some reason, because the next time he woke up it was broad day out and someone was banging pots and pans about somewhere in the house.

He propped himself up on one elbow, fumbled his watch from the vest draped over the bedside chair, and muttered, "Thunderation!" when he saw it was going on 9:00 A.M. There was no excuse for man or boy to sleep so late alone. So he got up, took a whore bath at the washstand in the corner, and hauled on his duds to catch up with the rest of the world.

Out in the kitchen he found Mary Lou Crimmins was the one making all the noise with her kitchen utensils. She greeted Longarm with a sweet, motherly smile and asked him what he wanted for breakfast. He saw that she had a big coffee pot ever simmering on the back of her kitchen range, so he allowed he could sure use some Arbuckle, but said he wasn't hungry. As she poured him a mug he asked what she was making in all those other pots and pans, for from the looks and smells she was stirring up enough for a harvest crew or an army.

The agent's wife said army was closer, adding that her husband and the Indian police were out hunting raiders together and she expected them back, hungry, by noon.

As he sat at her kitchen table sipping coffee, Longarm

didn't comment on her pessimism. He doubted they'd cut the raider's trail on sun-baked prairie, either. Nobody so far had been able to. But he found something more unusual to comment on. "I know this is none of my business, Miss Mary Lou, but at most agencies I've visited the white lady of the house generally has Indian servants."

The sweet-faced Mary Lou made an ugly face and replied, "I'd rather keep house my way than with the dubious help of unwashed squaws! My husband made the suggestion when we first came up here. But my mother raised me to keep house proper, not to laze about whilst surly serving girls sweep under the rug and neglect the cobwebs in the corners. As to letting Indians prepare *food,* forget it! They can't tell flour from sugar and they always leave out the salt."

Longarm nodded as if he agreed with her and finished his coffee without further comment. He wasn't the one doing all the work, so he felt no need to explain Plains Indian notions of cooking. More than one old squaw had told him how awful white gals cooked, too. He'd found that a man could eat almost anything, if he was a well-mannered dinner guest.

Longarm thanked his white hostess, left the mug in the dry sink, and went out to see what else he could find out about the way the agency was run. He'd told a white lie about not being hungry. He headed first to the trading post across the way to see if he could hit more than one bird with the same excuse.

It was gloomy, cluttered, and funny-smelling inside the low-roofed log structure. A pretty little Indian gal in a calico mother hubbard stared at him from behind the counter as he approached it, gasped as if she'd just seen a ghost, and ran into the back, whimpering in a mixture of bad French and what sounded like Algonquin. A few moments later a middle-aged gent with white features and Indian coloring came out, smiling, to say, "My Marie, he is scared of white men, she. I am Chambrun, and you must be the deputy they sent, *non?*"

Longarm nodded. "I am. My handle is Custis Long, and I sure could use a can of tomato preserves and some pemmican."

The breed sighed and replied, "Alas, I have neither for sale here, *mon ami!* The Blackfoot have simple tastes when it comes to vegetables. I have parched corn, beans in the sack, and in season a few squash or pumpkin taken in trade. No tinned tomato or, indeed, any tinned vegetation, *hein?*"

"What about the pemmican? Surely your Indian customers still eat pemmican."

"*Oui,* but they *make* it. They do not *buy* it. There is, as you may know, a meat packer back East who makes what some white people seem willing to call pemmican. I do not stock it. I am half Ojibwa, myself."

Longarm chuckled and said, "I follow your drift. But I'm still hungry as a wolf. I got some iron rations in my saddlebags over to the agency stable. But I had something more refreshing than iron in mind. So what would you suggest?"

Chambrun called out in his own mixed lingo before he told Longarm, "My woman keeps a bowl of trapper's stew going day and night. Perhaps if she salts a bowl to your taste you can get it down, *non?*"

"Why, that's neighborly as hell of you, Mr. Chambrun," Longarm said. "But I don't need extra salt. I've eaten Indian before and liked it."

So the trader laughed, opened the flap down at the end of the counter, and led Longarm back to his private quarters. As they entered the kitchen the little Miami gal was backed into a corner, looking scared, as Longarm removed his hat and smiled at her. Chambrun said something to her in their odd dialect and as both men sat down Marie overcame her fear or her shyness enough to put coffee in front of them both and serve Longarm a tin plate of trapper's stew. Chambrun had been right about it needing salt, but as Longarm dug in he said it was delicious. For it was, to Plains Indian taste. Over in the Great Basin, a Paiute housewife would have served it *too* salty for a white man's tongue. A traveling man learned that folk in different parts had different tastes. It'd be a mighty dull world if everyone, everywhere, agreed on everything, Longarm mused.

As Longarm demolished the stew, Chambrun took advantage of his obviously sophisticated palate to ask politely when he'd last enjoyed trapper's stew. Longarm said, "I was up Canada way a few months ago. I was trailing a white outlaw wanted here in the States. But I naturally met all sorts of Canadian folk, red, white, and Metis."

"Ah? And how did m'sieur get along with my *très* dangerous rebel distant relations?"

Longarm washed down some stew with black coffee before he replied. "Tolerable. I wasn't riding for the Mac-Donald administration and, so far, none of Louis Riel's guerrillas has robbed a U. S. bank to fund his separatist movement." He hesitated, then decided to put all the cards on the table. "Matter of fact, I met old Louis in the flesh. He acted like a gent, and so did I. That's likely why we're both alive and well this morning."

Chambrun blinked in surprise. "You *know* Louis Riel! *Eh bien,* tell me, what did you think of him?"

Longarm shrugged. "I didn't notice his horns and tail, if he has any. I went to see him to ask his help in tracking a white owlhoot through his rebel territory. He agreed him and his Metis had enough trouble with Canadian lawmen alone. So he passed the word it was not in the revolution's interest to gun a U. S. federal deputy in Canada without an entry permit or even the knowledge of Ottawa. I sort of liked old Louis Riel, as a matter of fact. He struck me a sensible enough cuss, despite his doomed dream."

Chambrun raised an eyebrow and asked, "Ah? You do not expect the Metis to win, then?"

Longarm shook his head soberly. "They ain't got the chance of a snowball in hell. Even with the poor whites and disgruntled full bloods there ain't enough fighting men in all of Western Canada to take on the British Empire."

Chambrun scowled and said, "Damn, their cause is *just,* you know! MacDonald's Tories had no right to grant railroaders the right of way across the hard-won homesteads of earlier settlers, white as well as Metis!"

Longarm drained the last of his coffee and leaned back. "The James boys said much the same about the Missouri Pacific Railroad. They might have been right, for all I know. But they ain't been *winning* lately. I had this same discussion with old Louis Riel himself. So, if it's all the same to you, I don't want to argue about the rights and wrongs of either side again. It ain't my fight, thank God."

Chambrun grinned sheepishly. "Nor mine. Forgive me, *mon ami,* it is foolish for a man who is now an American citizen to argue the Canadian Metis cause. It is just that . . . *Merde alors,* if only I could get my younger brother out of there. But, *non,* he insists our old homestead along the Red River is ours forever, by white as well as red law, and . . . Alas, you know how idealistic we all were at twenty-two, *non?*"

Longarm sighed. "I'd had some of my idealism shot out of me by twenty-two. The War was over just about the time I got old enough to vote. But I savvy your family problem. I won't suggest you talk your kid brother into coming south, since I know you've already tried. But that reminds me of

125

others who might want to move out of the war zone. Did you know many Cree to speak of, when you still lived up along the Red River?"

Chambrun grimaced and replied, "The agent, Crimmins, keeps asking me that same question. So has the army. Hear me: I am French and Ojibwa. My Marie, here, is a full-blood Miami, from the wild rice country even further east. Canada is a big country, bigger than these United States, and its high plains are wider once the Shining Mountains swing west to the north. If all of us dirty redskins were on closer speaking terms, neither I nor the white man's West would exist today. When my parents met, the Ojibwa were at peace with the Great White Mother in London, but the Cree were at war, and..."

"Let's not rehash ancient history, old son," Longarm said with a weary smile. "What's done is done, and I'm more interested in what's been going on *here,* more recent. Whether you know any Plains Cree personally or not, you're more Indian than me, so I'd like your opinion as to what might have driven the Cree south."

Chambrun shrugged and replied, "I have no idea. Neither do my Blackfoot customers. There are no buffalo on this reserve. There are buffalo, and white men's cows galore, up by the Peace River. But the Mounties are tough. Maybe the Cree feel safer raiding down this way, *non?"*

"I won't take that as insulting as the U. S. Army might, old son. But I fail to see that as a sensible motive. You forget I've rid across Canadian range and, to tell the truth, if I was a wild Indian just out for beef or hair, I'd feel safer raising hell on my own range, in more open country. There's twice as many well-armed settlers here in Montana and, worse yet, them mysterious raiders seem to have chosen mighty dangerous U.S. Indians as their particular target. It just don't make a lick of sense to me."

Chambrun said, "To me, either. But you are a white man, and I may think whiter than a Cree. In the Shining Times, the Blackfoot and Cree were not fond of one another, *hein?*"

"Yeah, but the Shining Times are over and, even if they wasn't, why in thunder should Cree be riding against the Blackfoot under a half-ass rebel banner? Even if the Plains Cree have joined Riel's rebellion, they ain't rebelling against the Blackfoot nation, damn it!"

Chambrun started to suggest something, then smiled sheepishly and said, *"Eh bien,* the waving of rebel banners makes the idea they have ridden south to avoid the troubles to the north *très* grotesque as well, *non?* I confess, *mon ami,* I have no idea what they came down here for!"

Longarm nodded. "I'd best get back to finding out, then. I thank you both for your kind hospitality. Your wife's stew will likely stick with me past noon. Does she savvy any English at all, pard?"

Chambrun shook his head and said Marie only knew French and Algonquin. So Longarm said he'd leave it to the trader to tell her how much he admired everything about her, and they parted friendly.

Outside, he spied old Snake Killer rocking on the porch of an unpainted pre-cut shanty. He walked over and sat on the steps at the old man's feet. He took out a couple of cheroots, lit his own, and held up the other one until Snake Killer took it silently and rocked a few more times. Then, as Longarm had hoped, the old chief lit up and enjoyed a few puffs before he said, conversationally, "This tobacco is not bad. If you want to know why I did not ride out with the young men and the blue sleeves this morning, they did not ask me to. That red-nosed captain of theirs thinks he knows so much. Hear me: They will find nothing, nothing. Captain Gatewood drinks too much to find anything."

Longarm blew a smoke ring, watched it drift out to the path in the sunlight, and said, "I thought I might drift up to where those two women and the boy were killed. I know my Blackfoot brothers would have found any sign the killers left, but I thought I'd have a look just the same." He blew another smoke ring. "I am waiting for someone to tell me where the place might be."

Snake Killer blew smoke up at the roof overhang and kept rocking as he softly observed, "This old man has nothing better to do right now. I think it might be fun to watch my young white son look for sign where keener eyes failed to see any. It is not far enough to be worth the task of saddling up. Come."

The old Indian rose and started walking. Longarm got up to follow. Snake Killer led him out of the settlement and across a modest stretch of prairie, to the mouth of a brush-choked draw. The old man stopped where the brush grew waist-high and unbuttoned his jeans to relieve himself. Longarm figured he might as well do the same. As they stood there, Snake Killer asked, "If you are so smart, why have not the women taken all this brush for firewood, so close to home?"

Longarm said, "It would be foolish to cut wild cherry when cottonwood and willow burn as well and offer no fruit, wouldn't it?"

Snake Killer buttoned his fly. He nodded grudgingly and said, "At least you can tell wild cherry from willow, even now, with the fruit picked off for the year. Come. The place you seek is further up the wash."

As they moved single file along the narrow path between the rank unpruned choke cherry bushes, for hardly any had grown high enough to be called trees, Longarm noticed a half-dried cherry here and there among the fluttering leaves. "This draw has been flash-flooded within the last ten summers, I see," he said.

Snake Killer sounded disgusted as he replied, "Tell a grandfather how long it takes wild cherry to grow back from the stump. I agree it's a bothersome tangle. But, on the other hand, there is more fruit to be gathered with so many new sprouts, tangled as they are. The women who got killed must have hoped for better picking further up. As you can see, most of the fruit has been picked, and what is left is starting to go bad."

They forged almost a mile up the draw as the banks rose steeper and the going failed to improve. Then old Snake Killer punched through the entangled cherry branches to a flat expanse of summer-killed buffalo grass and stopped, saying, "This is where they found the two women and the boy. I am going to sit down in the shade. I looked for sign here yesterday."

Suiting actions to his words, the old Indian moved on to a taller-than-usual cherry tree above the little clearing and sat down, leaning his back against the trunk. Having finished the gift cheroot by now, he proceeded to roll his own, pretending not to be interested as Longarm stood staring down at the dead grass the dead Indians had been found on.

He naturally saw dried blood on many a straw stem, but he knew better than to comment on it. Nothing lighter than an elephant would have left footprints in the adobe-hard soil sodded thick as two welcome mats with wire-tough bleached straw. Longarm commenced to circle the grassy patch, examining the branches of the surrounding wild cherry. Snake Killer tried to keep quiet, but once he had his new smoke going he couldn't help telling it, "Hear me. We *looked* for broken branches. We found none. The raiders had plenty of time to work their way through it carefully. They must have been waiting here for the cherry pickers. They killed them, carved them, and left without leaving sign. There are no horse droppings on the high ground above this wash.

They moved in, far, on foot. Then they left the same way. They were good, for such cowardly squaw killers."

Longarm came over to hunker in the same modest shade as he observed, "They must have been fortune tellers, too, if it happened the way you tell it. I can see a war party sneaking across open prairie near a settlement if they did so before dawn. I can see them slipping down here without busting up all that brush, if they had reason. But what reason did they have?"

Snake Killer frowned and asked, "Have you not paid any attention to any of us, Longarm? They killed and scalped two women and a boy! They took the boy's private parts as well, and the white medicine man the agent got to examine all the dead said the women had been raped. Did you think those Cree came here to pick cherries?"

"No, and I fail to see why they expected anyone else up this far to pick 'em, either. There's something we're missing here, old son. The fruit picking season was over, officially. So, sure, *we* know ambitious cherry pickers come this far up the wash, but how could others, strangers in these parts, have *expected* cherry pickers this late in the year?"

Snake Killer nodded grudgingly. "Heya, that is a big queer. They had no other reason to be here when our people stumbled over them. They built no fire here. They did not have their ponies down in this wash, and you are right about the fruit being almost gone. Maybe they meant to creep down the wash through the brush, to dash out at the agency itself?"

Longarm pursed his lips thoughtfully and said, "Not by broad day across that stretch of open ground they'd still have to cross. If they meant to wait until dark, why bother? They could have hit, mounted, just as well from any direction. What time of the day were the bodies discovered here?"

Snake Killer glanced skyward. "Late afternoon. Maybe

four or five, as you count such positions of the sun. They had been up here since about noon. When they did not return to start preparing their husband's supper, he came looking for them. He found them naked and scalped, along with the boy, his nephew. He ran screaming back to the Indian police, of course. I came later, along with the other, wiser men. But we found no sign. Now you have found no sign. Can we go back now?"

Longarm shook his head. "It's hot everywhere right now. Did you just say both gals had one husband?"

Snake Killer hesitated, then said, "I should have put that differently. Your people have such silly laws. Fish Head was only married to the older woman of the two, as far as the B.I.A. ration books are concerned. The younger one was her sister. According to our own laws—"

"Say no more," Longarm cut in. "I understand your customs and it's not for me to judge 'em. So, all right, this Fish Head's two women come up here with a younger kinsman, and all three got killed. Did I meet this Fish Head at the powwow earlier?"

"No. He is in mourning, of course. It feels bad to lose two wives and a nephew all at once, even when you have someone you can kill to make their ghosts feel better. Fish Head follows the old ways, like me. Right now he must be carving tears of blood from his arms. That is the right way for a man to cry."

Longarm nodded and said, "So much for questioning him right now. He likely couldn't tell me anything you others can't, in any case. Tell me about the dead women, his two wives."

"There is little to say about them. They were both good persons. Like Fish Head, they followed the old ways. Neither had any children by him. Fish Head is not a young man and neither were they. The oldest wife was over thirty

131

as you count age. The younger was old, too. At least twenty-five."

"How about the boy who died with them? How old was he?"

"A baby. He was born after the Shining Times. So he never had the chance to count coup or seek visions. The poor boy died before he even had his adult name. We still called him Running Rabbit. He was good at children's games. In time he might have become a good man. It makes me very cross to think about it."

Longarm grimaced and said, "His four spirits are likely annoyed as hell, too. I wish one of 'em at least would tell me what happened here. Taking the scalps of women and children is bad enough, but the boy was treated plain disgusting. You still ain't said how old he was, in years, I mean."

Snake Killer shrugged. "We do not count the stages of our lives in years as your people do. He was a mere child, I tell you. Let me think. . . . He was born during the time you white people had the big fight between the blue sleeves and gray sleeves. Is that any help?"

Longarm nodded. "Yeah, that would put his age at anywhere between fifteen and twenty. That's old enough for the men who killed him to have taken him for a full-fledged Blackfoot brave. That still leaves us with the mystery of how they could have expected to meet any Blackfoot at all in such an out-of-the-way spot. Would the three of 'em have mentioned where they was headed to, say, the folk at the trading post?"

Snake Killer smiled thinly. "Rain Crow already thought of that. They didn't. They didn't say anything about coming up here to pick cherries to anyone but Fish Head himself. Fish Head told Rain Crow they left his cabin directly for this spot with their gathering baskets. He watched them go.

He says they stopped to talk to nobody as they left the settlement."

"What happened to their picking baskets? I don't see any baskets around here right now, do you?"

Snake Killer frowned and said, "Of course you don't. They had neither their clothes nor anything else when Fish Head found them, naked and dead!"

"You mean the killers rode off with baskets and the duds of Blackfoot women as well? What in hell for?"

"How should I know? Do I look like a squaw-killing Cree? What difference does it make where the dead people's things are now?"

Longarm stood up. "A lot of difference, if I find anyone else with 'em," he said. "Come on. I got to talk to Fish Head, in mourning or not. I aim to write down just what sort of duds and baskets we're talking about. Then, when I find 'em, I'll sure ask the ones I find 'em with a mess of serious questions!"

Chapter 12

They wouldn't let him talk to Fish Head. A medicine man came out of the old brave's cabin to warn how dangerous it was for a white man to pester an Indian in communication with the spirits. When Longarm gently insisted, the medicine man said, "Hear me: The dead people are with the old grandmother in her lodge beneath the northern lights, and part of Fish Head is visiting with them. I can tell you what you wish to know. I am Weasel Eyes. I know everyone and never forget anything. The older woman had on a red calico dress with white dots. Her younger sister wore blue of the same pattern the day she died. The boy, Running Rabbit, died dressed in blue jeans and a gray hickory shirt with white man's shoes, not moccasins, and he never wore a hat. The baskets you seek were not Indian made. They were just the strawberry picking baskets they sell at the trading post. None of our women seem to want to take the time to do things right any more. Have my words helped you, my white son?"

Longarm sighed and said, "Not as much as I'd hoped. Riding off with such nondescript trade goods makes even less sense." He turned to Snake Killer to ask, "Are you certain the stuff wasn't just tossed in the bush up there, out of easy sight?"

Snake Killer shook his head. "If it had been, we would have found it. Our best eyes searched every inch of the ground, from the clearing to the rims of the wash and beyond. They found nothing, nothing, not even a spot where a man might have scraped his knee hard, climbing out. The Cree took even their shadows with them, without leaving sign. Heya, they were *good,* the no-good dog-eating cowards!"

Longarm thanked them both for such little information as they'd provided him, and headed back to the agent's house. As he passed the trading post he spied a Blackfoot kid coming out with a fresh chaw of tobacco. The kid's face was familiar. Longarm stopped him and asked, "Ain't you one of Little Moon's cowhands, Pard?"

The kid sighed and said, "Yes. It's not fair. I wanted to ride after the Cree with the older boys, but Little Moon said we younger ones had to stay here and watch the agency herd."

Longarm gazed about and saw nothing but unpainted housing and an old woman carrying a pair of water buckets in the middle distance.

"They are out on the range, of course," the kid said. "My brothers are watching."

"Rank has its privileges, eh?" Longarm smiled, adding, "Tell me something. How many head of cows are we discussing, before and after the raids started?"

The boy frowned. "We have maybe two hundred and fifty here at the main agency. Other stations on other parts of reservation have their own herds, of course."

"Maybe ain't good enough, but I reckon it'll have to do for now. In the same round numbers, how many head did you have before some were run off on you?"

"Two hundred and fifty. We always keep about same number here."

Longarm frowned and said, "No offense, pard, but that don't make sense, even counting Indian style. How in thunder could anyone lose cows and wind up with the same number?"

The boy grinned, fresh as most his awkward age, and said, "Easy. The agent buys new cows to replace the ones the Cree take. If you white men are so smart, how come you ask such dumb questions?"

"It ain't easy. Let's try it another way. How many cows, all told, have been stolen?"

"Why didn't you ask that in the first place? About a hundred altogether. They took no cows yesterday when they killed Running Rabbit and the two old women."

Longarm nodded and was about to ask if the raiders had averaged the same number of head in each of their more neighborly actions when they both heard a bugle and turned to see the cavalry troop riding in under a cloud of dust and behind a screen of Indian scouts. The agent, Crimmins, was smart enough to ride point, ahead of the dust. They all seemed headed for Crimmins's house, so that was where Longarm headed.

He got there just as Crimmins and Captain Gatewood had dismounted and were clumping up the steps. Miss Mary Lou held the door open, smiling sweet as ever. Longarm followed them in as the lesser folk outside made do with the afternoon sun and shade as best they could. The agent's wife herded the three of them into her kitchen and sat them down for coffee and beans while Crimmins and Gatewood filled Longarm in on the results of their patrol.

The results hadn't resulted in much. Their Indians had found plenty of sign near the place where Longarm and the redhead had been jumped. But after riding off to the west in a bunch, the night riders had split up in every direction and, as Gatewood explained, trying not to cuss in front of a lady, tracking one pony across a well-traveled range was a pure waste of time. He added, "Most of the prairie's hard as a brick this time of year, and the few soft patches are trampled by a whole infernal tribe of Friendlies. One unshod pony leaves much the same sign as any other, even before

136

cows, dogs, and whatever stomp across it."

Longarm said he'd scouted for Hostiles in his day. He turned to Crimmins, and said, "I understand you've been replacing the herd as fast as it's been stolen?"

Crimmins nodded. "Have to. It's an eating herd, not a market herd."

Longarm asked him where he'd been getting the fresh beef.

Crimmins thought and said, "It's all come from local spreads. I could look up the exact numbers from each outfit if it's important. The paperwork's in my office."

Longarm shook his head and said, "It don't likely matter if the new beef ain't from a single source. I'd be insulting you if I asked you if you'd checked the brands before paying, right?"

Crimmins laughed incredulously. "Every head I've purchased since I've been here has been branded Interior Department on delivery, of course. If you're asking whether or not I'd be stupid enough to buy beef already wearing that big ID on its hide, you're right. It's insulting."

Gatewood laughed. "The army hasn't been buying Indian beef of late, either. Ours comes branded Big U, Big S. You're not the first one who's thought of that angle, Longarm. We've checked with the brand inspector in town as well. Nobody's been shipping beef from these parts branded with anything an artist with a running iron could make out of that big government brand."

Longarm nodded. "That saves me a dumb conversation at the loading pens in town, then. But the raiders must have herded the purloined cows *somewhere*. If they were slaughtering 'em on the prairie to feed one mighty big band, the Blackfoot as well as the carrion crows should have noticed by now. There's just no way to butcher that many head without leaving sign. So what's left?"

Gatewood said, "They're not going over the mountains

to the west. The few passes have been checked out. The white outfits to the south are already arguing over water holes and rights of way, so a strange herd would have attracted considerable attention, even if the drovers weren't dressed up like hostile Indians. That leaves Canada, where the infernal Cree come from in the first place."

Longarm frowned thoughtfully. "Aside from sounding like a fool's errand, it don't work. Both the Indian police and you yellow legs have been trying to head 'em off south of the border and, so far, nobody's been able to cut sign. Since I admire both the Indian police and the U. S. Army, I'm convinced they can't be streaking back and forth from the logical direction. It ain't logical they ain't been caught at it by now."

"Thanks, I think," Gatewood said. "But back up and tell us why you think it's so foolish for Canadian Cree to jump the border for beef. So far they've been gathering an awful lot of the same down here!"

Longarm nodded, but said, "They raise beef north of the border, too. With the Metis revolt going on up there, the situation should be lots more unsettled than down here. The Mounties and the Canadian militia are too busy chasing Louis Riel's guerrilla bands to guard outlying cattle spreads. So why in thunder would any cow thieves, red *or* white, be down here doing it the harder way? And how come these mystery raiders have only been hitting the herds of other Indians? That big government brand makes it nigh impossible to ever hide the Blackfoot beef, even in Canada. While at the same time, I know of more than one small white spread within a day's ride where the pickings would be a deal safer. The late Roping Sally ran her Lazy W between here and town with only a handful of part-time help. Many a local nester keeps a few head of stock with no hired help at all. See what I mean?"

Crimmins nodded and said, "We're way ahead of you again, Longarm. It's obvious the Cree are making war on my Blackfoot wards in particular. The tribal elders tell me the feud's been going on for centuries. We agree that the Cree have been taking advantage of unsettled conditions in Canada to settle old scores, but for once the army and the B.I.A. are in complete agreement, and the Cree are in for one dismal surprise."

Captain Gatewood smiled like a mean little kid and said, "That's for sure. The War Department's lending the B.I.A. the wherewithal to dismal the daylights out of those raiders. The batteries should be here some time this evening."

"Batteries?" asked Longarm with a puzzled frown.

The captain explained, "Gatling guns. Six for my outfit at Fort Banyon and another half dozen for the Indian police here. I'll naturally detail army instructors to show the Indians how to use 'em. But how long can it take even an Indian to learn how to turn a crank?"

Crimmins nodded and said, "In a day or so we should be well set up, with a hot reception posted all around this agency. The captain here assures me that one gatling gun crew can mow down any number of raiders as determined as they come!"

"A thousand rounds a minute, if you really whip the crank around." Gatewood grinned, adding, "Of course, that's one of the fine details we mean to teach the Indians before we turn 'em loose with gatlings. No sense running out of ammo by firing too fast. The nice thing about a gatling is that she'll fire anywhere from single shot to buzz-saw. War's sending plenty of ammo, of course. But we got to act sensible, and..." He trailed off as he saw that Longarm was scraping back from the table to rise.

"This is all mighty interesting, folks, but I have to get back into town and send me some wires," Longarm said.

Crimmins rose with him, frowning. "You can wire anyone you like from right here, Longarm. Didn't you know I have a telegraph set spliced into the cross-country Western Union network?"

Longarm nodded. "Most Indian agencies as well as army posts do. But I got a mess of messages to get off."

"I could send 'em for you free."

"So could I. I learned how to work the key in my army days, pard. But I don't have to pay Western Union out of my own pocket, and it makes no sense for you or me to spend so much time tapping like woodpecker birds when Western Union has so many men better at it working for 'em by the hour. Besides, there could be some messages waiting for me in town."

Crimmins shrugged and told him to suit himself. Longarm nodded, but then he said, "Hold the thought. As long as you're so anxious to play with your telegraph set, would you like to join me in an electrical experiment?"

Crimmins looked blank. Longarm went on, "They tell me in town that the wire from Switchback to Ford MacLeod, Canada, is out of order. Could we try and reach the Mounties from here?"

Crimmins agreed it was worth a try and led the way to the cellar steps and down to his telegraph setup. Longarm didn't ask why he'd moved it down to the root cellar. Few house-proud wives would approve of battery jars filled with acid in the neater parts of the house. Crimmins fumbled in the dark for some matches, lit a candle, and switched on the set, saying, "I leave it shut down when I'm not at home. Saves the battery plates."

"How do you know when messages are incoming, with the set down here?"

Crimmins pointed to an ingeniously wired door buzzer on the desk. "This rings to wake the dead when it's on the line. It's not now. So who do you want me to try to the north? Someone named MacLeod?"

Longarm said he'd better do it, and Crimmins didn't object as he sat down at the key. He tapped out the call numbers for Fort MacLeod and waited a spell. He was just about to observe that the line was still dead when the Canadian operator tapped back. Longarm grinned. "The Western Union crew must have found the break this very day, for they couldn't get through last night." Then he tapped out his message to Crown Sergeant Foster at Fort MacLeod and added that he'd pick up the answer at the Switchback Western Union office.

Crimmins said, "You sure have a fast fist, Longarm. What was that about the Mounties staking out some place called Whisky Gap?"

"You got a good ear, too. Whisky Gap's where *I'd* cross the border in a hurry and in numbers, with mayhaps some cows keeping me company. In case I tapped it out too fast for you near the end, me and Foster have worked together in the past. We save words by skipping the ones we both know. When he gets my message he'll get my full meaning and wire me back just how serious they're taking old Louis Riel this summer."

He could tell Crimmins had lots of other questions to ask. But he got up and headed out to get his horse more sudden than was polite, only pausing on the stairs to say, "I got to get cracking. You may have noticed they sent me up here short-handed, and this case is about to bust wide open."

Chapter 13

The ride into town didn't take too long. But since electric current moved a lot faster than a chestnut mare, Longarm found that Crown Sergeant Foster's reply from Canada had beaten him to the Switchback Western Union by a good twenty minutes. As the clerk handed it over, along with other messages from other parts, Longarm asked him when the wire crews had located the break on the prairie, and where.

The clerk said, "They never did. Canada just come back on the line recent, without our help. The cut must have been north of the border and the Canadian crews must have repaired it."

Longarm scanned the message from the Mounties. "If they did, it's sure curious Fort MacLeod don't mention it," he remarked. "Wire 'em back and ask 'em how long they've been out of touch with the States. I don't have to write down such a simple message, do I?"

The clerk allowed he was curious, too. So while Longarm read the wires from other, stateside lawmen, the clerk contacted his opposite number north of the line for an informal chat. Longarm had just stuffed the last answer to his earlier queries away when the clerk returned to the counter.

"That's funny," he told the lawmen. "Canada says they didn't know they'd been cut off from the States at all. They've been sending and receiving regular, albeit not heavy, with the country out this way so empty on both sides of the line. I asked if they'd tried to send any earlier wires to this

142

particular office and they said they hadn't, so that might explain it."

Longarm frowned thoughtfully, picked up a pencil from the counter, and wrote another message to Fort MacLeod, asking his old Mountie pals if they recalled an earlier difference of opinion on jurisdiction and begging Foster to forgive him as he'd surely forgive *him* if it ever happened again. The clerk scanned the message, said it sure read funny, but that he'd send it. Longarm told him not to be so hasty, as he had another urgent message for the law in Middle Fork, Dakota Territory. So the clerk waited until Longarm wrote out suggestions for another stakeout and then sat down to send them both.

Longarm still had to study some before he wired Billy Vail about a more delicate matter. He rode over to the livery to leave his mount to her oats and water before getting any needled beer for his brain.

The young stable boy on duty at Bonnie's livery said he'd be proud to take care of the hired nag. But as Longarm tipped him a nickel and turned to leave a familiar voice called out from the rear, "Custis Long, you come right back here, you mean old thing!"

He went back between the stalls to confront the redhead, now dressed more sedately in a calico dress.

"I mean to have a word with you in private," Bonnie said. "Let's go back to my quarters again, you brute."

The bedroom looked just about the same by daylight. Bonnie had changed her bed linens since they'd rumpled them, but the gin bottle was still in place, though almost empty, now.

"I must have had a mite too much to drink last night," she said. "For the next I knew I was all alone in the dark, and where were *you*, you fool?"

He sighed and said, "Feeling foolish, alone on the prairie.

143

I snuffed your candle on the way out lest you set yourself on fire, thrashing. You did get mighty drunk, I fear."

She laughed sheepishly. "I've been trying all day to remember what else I may or may not have gotten. I can't think of a delicate way to put it. Did we or didn't we?"

He tried not to laugh as he assured her soberly, "You don't have to worry, Red. I've always considered rolling drunks for money or anything else disgusting."

"Now he tells me," she sighed. "After I've already taken precautions." She scowled up at him and added, "Are you saying you thought I was too disgusting to make love to, you bastard?"

"My folks was married, Red. But I would have been a bastard, had I taken advantage of a sleeping beauty, tempting as she might have been."

Bonnie reached up, rémoved his hat, and hauled him in for a loving hug as she said flatly, "Well, I'm not asleep now, damn it. So what have you got to say for yourself?"

"Powder River and let her buck!" He laughed, hugging her back as they fell all the way down to the mattress together. But as he ran a hand up her bare thigh beneath her thin skirts Bonnie said, "Not with our clothes and a gun rig on, damn it! Let me lock the door and get us both bare, first. I told you last night I ain't had any for a coon's age, and now that I've got you, I mean to get you *right!*"

So she did. As Longarm undressed, Bonnie shucked her dress and sat down to take off her shoes as naturally and unblushing as if they'd been together for a month or more. But there was nothing cut and dried about the way she rubbed her bare hide all over his once they got started. They did it old-fashioned to break the ice, with her coming three times ahead of him. Then she said she wanted to get on top, so he let her. It made a lot of sense when one considered the difference in their sizes. The bitty redhead was tough enough to take Longarm's full weight in her love saddle, and eager enough to enjoy it, but it was true she could move faster, crouched over him with her sassy little rump gyrating in every direction as she literally screwed her way up and down his excited shaft.

She laughed and said, "I felt that!" as he ejaculated up into her. Then she started moving faster, growled sort of cute, and added, "I'm not about to let you off so easy! Your red-headed momma's been waiting a long time for a boy as young and innocent to take home and raise, and I must allow you sure raise good! Oh, it feels so goooood!"

It must have, to her, but Longarm was feeling a mite left out as she collapsed in a weak cuddly pile atop him, pulsating in pleasure on his re-inspired erection. He rolled her over, spread her little shapely thighs wide, and proceded to finish right as Bonnie gasped, "Take it *easy!* You're hitting bottom with every stroke, and ... Never mind what I just said. I love it, and I'm coming again!"

That made two of them that time. It was good to see that their bodies were starting to work in team so soon. But when all good things came to an end for the moment, and he dismounted for a smoke and, hopefully, his second wind, Bonnie buried her red head in his bare shoulder and sobbed, "Oh, my God, whatever must you think of me now?"

He held her closer, fumbling for his shirt on the floor beside the bed with his free hand. "Up to now, I've been thinking mighty well of you, Red. Do we have to go through that usual afterwards stuff?"

She sniffed and said, "I don't know what came over me just now. I've never thrown myself at a man in such a shameless fashion before."

He saw that, yeah, they had to go through the same old afterwards stuff. So he fumbled out a cheroot and a light and started blowing smoke rings at the ceiling as she went on about how lonesome she'd been since she'd been widowed and how tedious the gents were here in this little one-horse town. It was good to hear, at least, how discreet she was. Since it only seemed to be passing strangers who swept her off her feet, he probably didn't have to worry about her uncle the sheriff hearing unseemly gossip about a fellow lawman. In fact, Bonnie made him promise he'd never tell a soul about what had just happened, to her total surprise and chagrin, adding that she'd just die if word got about that she was a wayward widow woman. He found it easy to swear he'd never brag on his seduction of her. That was what she called it—a seduction. Nobody screwed that good without considerable practice.

But, what the hell, the old lady down at the far end of town had told the sheriff those four gunslicks who'd hired mounts from Bonnie had been staying at her boarding house. So nobody else by whom the redhead had been taken advantage of recently mattered, unless they looked like Indians. He didn't think he'd better ask her about that. It was unlikely as well as impolite.

She was right about it being hard to get laid discreetly in a small town, and someone would surely have noticed if what appeared to be the Cree nation had been hanging about the livery stable lately.

His mind followed the smoke rings to more interesting heights as the naked redhead snuggled against him, protesting her more usual innocence while he toyed absently with her sweet little tail-bone between her firm bare buttocks. He knew he wouldn't be getting any answers to the latest wires he'd sent for a spell. He would worry about the one he hoped he wouldn't be sending to Denver after Lansford in Middle Fork informed him whether his hunch about the black-bannered ship tattooed on a dead man's chest was right or not. Nobody had it on any Wanted posters on either

146

side of the border. But the dead man had obviously served in some navy at some time and, while he couldn't be sure, Longarm had seen that vessel or one a lot like it framed over many a bar, farther south. He doubted there'd be a similar print anywhere here in Switchback, unfortunately. They were too far inland as well as too far north to be interested in sea battles of the Sixties.

He blew another smoke ring, then asked Bonnie, "Is there a library here in Switchback, honey?"

She raised her head from his shoulder. "What's that supposed to mean, you brute?"

He said, "Just what it sounds like. A library is a place where they keep books and prints. I'm looking for a picture of a steam-oxed full-rigged ship, converted to serious from a merchant vessel. I wired the law in Middle Fork I *thought* it could be the Confederate raider *Alabama*. But I'd feel better if I knew for certain."

She started toying with his sated shaft, women being like that, as she asked him why on earth he was interested in naval architecture at a time like this. He pulled her well-designed foundations closer to him and he chuckled fondly. "If that gent your uncle gunned last night was so proud of having served in the Confederate navy he tattooed the old *Alabama* across his chest, it hardly seems likely he could have been a Canadian. On the other hand, the vessel's flag had been blacked out, and the British have a tolerable-sized navy, too. I'd know better if I could study a print of the *Alabama* to make sure."

She started pumping harder with her skilled hand. "Are you tired of me already, Custis?" she asked.

He snuffed out the cheroot. "Not hardly. But I thought you was mad at me for taking advantage of a woman alone, little darling."

She sighed. "I am. You should be ashamed of yourself.

But now that the damage has been done, could you think me worse if I gave in to your unbridled lust again?"

He said, "I reckon not. What sort of disgusting demands do you want me to make on you next, Red?"

They didn't have a library in town, and the schoolhouse was closed for the day by the time Bonnie Murphy let Longarm stop abusing her. He said he'd try to get back to abuse her some more after sundown, but not to hold him to it. She said he was horrid. He didn't ask whether she meant he was horrid because he'd laid her or because he might not be back to lay her some more. Bonnie made more sense in a gunfight than anywhere else.

At the Western Union office, he found out he didn't have to look for a print of the old *Alabama*. The law he had alerted over in Middle Fork had just left a message for him, thanking him kindly for his warning that one or more total strangers might appear in town from nowhere to look up the old girl friend of the late Hard-Ass Henry Harrison. Lansford had staked out the whorehouse and, indeed, a pair of gents named Johnson and Green had walked into the trap, unaware that the loot from the U.P. robbery had been recovered. The one calling himself Johnson had lived long enough to curse everyone considerably and request that his body be shipped back to his kin in Georgia, who seemed to be named Thurgood, not Johnson, for some reason. Otherwise, Middle Fork had nothing new to add about the mysterious white-hatted gang Longarm had been brushing with of late. But what they'd sent him was enough.

As Longarm strode back out into the late afternoon sunlight, Sheriff Murphy stopped him to say, "You're looking mighty pleased with yourself today, Longarm. Where are you headed to celebrate what? If it's the saloon, I'll go with you."

Longarm chuckled. "I am feeling sort of smart for a change. But right now I got to look up the local brand inspector. Would you happen to know where he lives?" he asked.

Murphy nodded. "I'll go with you. It ain't far. I wanted a word with you in private, anyway. There's a delicate family matter we'd best get out in the open."

To change the subject fast, Longarm said, "We don't have to worry about them rascals in white hats no more, Sheriff. I just found out who they were and why they were after me. It had nothing to do with you all in these parts. The other night I questioned a sidekick of theirs and he got loose-lipped about some holdup loot. They knew I knew where it might be, so they were trying to nail me before I could finish up here and go look for it. The fools never considered that we lawmen communicate by wire instead of the hard way these days. So it's all over save for a few last tidy-ups that can wait. I'm sure sorry I suggested they could be Canadians or something trying to look like American hands in brand-new duds. Harrison and all his sidekicks were Southerners who've been dressing cow for some time. They just changed into new clothes because they knew witnesses had described them in their old outfits. When a man holds up a train wearing a beat-up dark hat, he just naturally wants to be seen the next time wearing a new white one, and—"

"Never mind all that. Who was it I shot last night, and is there any money out on the son of a bitch?" the sheriff asked.

"I can't tell you his true name," said Longarm, adding, "Records of the Confederate Navy ain't all that complete these days. But if anyone wanted serious had been running about with a full-rigged ship tattooed on his chest we'd have had him on our current yellow sheets. The whole gang was

149

small potatoes, save for Harrison himself, and he's long gone. Real pros wouldn't have acted so crazy. But they were just fools, so we can forget 'em. Right now I'm after bigger game."

"The house you're looking for is around the next corner," said Murphy. "Before we get there, I want to talk to you about my niece, Bonnie."

Longarm didn't answer.

Murphy said, "My sister done her best to raise that gal proper. But as you may have noticed, Bonnie's sort of forward."

"Do tell? I've been sort of busy looking for more suspicious characters, Sheriff."

"I hope so. For Bonnie's been spoken for by a gent who's suspicious as hell about anyone hanging around her. He's a top hand at the Slash K and just last month I barely managed to stop him from stomping a traveling salesman all the way to death. You see, he only gets into town once a week, and his intended being so flirty as well as handsome—"

"He has a problem," Longarm cut in, keeping his voice less interested than he had any right to feel. "I'll hopefully be gone before Saturday night. Meanwhile, as we seem to be talking growed-up man to growed-up man, has there been any gossip about me and Bonnie I should know about?"

Murphy sighed. "Nobody has to spread gossip about my sister's crazy red-headed daughter, damn it. It's an established fact that if there's a good-looking single man in town, Bonnie makes a play for him. You're here. You've been seen riding in off the dark lone prairie with the gal, and you've been doing other business with her since you arrived. Don't tell me if she's trifled with you yet or not. I don't want to know. You're bigger than me, and her boy friend out to the Slash K is bigger than both of us put together.

They call him Jumbo, and it's only a slight exaggeration."

"I'll keep it in mind I don't want to meet him, then. Let's talk about more sensible things, like cattle brands and bills of sale."

As luck would have it, the cattle brand inspector was sitting on his front porch, shelling peas, when the sheriff led Longarm to him and introduced them. The older man nodded pleasantly and said, "Got to help the old woman around the house since our daughter run off to get hitched. What do you need to know about brands, son? My books is over to my office by the railroad, but I don't need 'em to tell you there ain't been a new brand registered in recent memory."

Longarm braced a boot on the steps and asked, "Do you have any brands on file at all that could look anything at all like a run ID?"

The old man popped a pod and shook his head. "Already been over that same ground with the army and the B.I.A., son. I can see by your outfit that you know the cattle industry, so you must know it's the big, simple brands that are hardest to run. Most of our local outfits use stamp brands, since even an honest stockman has been known to have trouble explaining a simple burglar's tool. There's no brand in these parts that could be burnt over that big government brand without folks questioning its artistry. If you need further discouragement, like I told them other boys, there ain't been cow one shipped out of Switchback since them raids on the Blackfoot reserve commenced just a few days ago. Last serious beef leaving here was this spring. Won't be any more going out this side of the fall roundup next month. High summer's a tedious part of the year for me. Do you like peas for supper?"

Longarm declined the invitation graciously and said, "I've one more question. The Indian agency must have replaced its stolen beef from nearby spreads, right?"

The brand inspector nodded. "So I hear. I only officiates in such matters when the ownership of a critter could be in possible dispute. The talk about the stockyards is that the agency bought stock a head here and a head there from here and there. None of the men as sold stock recent to the Indians enjoys a rep for shady business practices or sudden increases to their modest herds, if that's what you're getting at." He popped another pea pod and added, "I may be old, but I can still ride, and my eyes still work. So I can tell you true there ain't been any Indian beef in or out of Switchback, recent or any other time. That big ID brand is just too hard to run."

Longarm said he would take the brand inspector's word for it, and left with Murphy to study further over needled beer. Longarm saw that they could have made a bad move as soon as they entered the saloon. For the sun was going down outside and, inside, a gent dressed cow at the far end of the bar was brushing dust from the ceiling beams with his Stetson—and he didn't wear his hat high-crowned.

The giant nodded pleasantly enough at Murphy. The sheriff gulped and said, "Evening, Jumbo. We wasn't expecting you in town so early in the week."

"The boss sent me in to study some cows," Jumbo said.

"You missing any stock, Jumbo?"

"Nope. We was told another outfit wants to get rid of some cheap. They was supposed to be here by now with a market herd of mixed scrub. Who's your little friend, Murph?"

The sheriff introduced Longarm and, since the giant wanted to shake, Longarm had to. It didn't hurt as much as Jumbo was trying to make it hurt. Longarm knew enough to jam the web of his thumb hard against that of a bigger man so he would have no real leverage as he set out to crush

Longarm's knuckles. He could tell by the suddenly thoughtful look in the big ramrod's pale blue eyes that Jumbo found his own grip a mite uncomfortable. Longarm only dug his thumb into the bones like that when he was shaking with a natural bully.

Jumbo smiled thinly and said, "I can tell you've done some hard roping in your day, Deputy. Mebbe you'd like to advise us about the beef the boss is interested in, if it ever gets here."

They let go of one another's throbbing paws and bellied side by side to the bar with Longarm between the giant and the sheriff. Murphy held up three fingers to the barkeep. "I hadn't heard of any pending beef trades, Jumbo," he told his niece's fiancé. "Since my jurisdiction covers this entire country, I'm a mite chagrined to hear of it so late, too. Who's thinning his herd at such a peculiar time of the year?"

Jumbo said, "Outfit calt the Triple Eight. One county line south or, to be exact, they're running a feeding operation on a modest spread surrounded by federal range. As we got their tale of woe, they've been stuffing scrub with their own water and Uncle Sam's grass, hoping to make a killing during the fall beef sales. But the killings over to the Blackfoot agency has 'em worried, so they want to get out of the game while they're still ahead."

Longarm picked up the schooner the barkeep slid his way. "Ain't *you* worried about Indian trouble, Jumbo?" he asked.

The young giant laughed. "Not hardly. That ain't bragging. The Indians ain't hit one white outfit yet and, when and if they ever do, the Slash K ain't the one it would be smart to start with. We're betting them scrub feeders is overcautious. But if they ain't, let the damned Cree come at a real outfit. I rid agin' the Sioux in Seventy-seven, and it was lots of fun."

Longarm didn't see fit to point out how much fun it might have been in Seventy-six, when the Indians had been winning. He said, "We just now came from the brand inspector's place, and it's odd he never mentioned word one of a big cattle sale, Jumbo."

Jumbo shrugged and said, "No reason he should have. Ain't no spreads around here *missing* any cows. The onliest stock them Cree run off was Indian beef. They ain't even hit the Triple Eight, yet. So the only suspicious thing about the transaction is that they ain't here yet and, damn it, I was hoping to have more time with my true love in town this evening!"

Longarm wouldn't have said a word, but Murphy asked, in a desperately casual voice, "Have you and Bonnie set the date yet, Jumbo?"

Jumbo shook his head morosely. "She keeps putting me off for some reason. I've tolt that little gal time and again she's mine and I mean to hear no more about it, but I reckon she's just shy."

Longarm felt better about the girl he'd spent most of the afternoon with as he grasped her problem better. It was small wonder the poor little gal was lonely, with an ogre like this one scaring off all the local Prince Charmings. He wondered if old Jumbo had ever even kissed her. He didn't think he'd better ask.

The sun and the beer were sinking seriously when they all heard the thuds of hoofbeats and the jingle of harness outside. Jumbo growled, "It's about time, God damn it! Do you boys reckon they're trying to green me in the dark with worthless scrub?"

"Things like that do happen," Longarm agreed as he and the sheriff followed Jumbo outside.

But it wasn't a trail herd reining in out front. It was a troop of cavalry led by Captain Gatewood along with the

154

Indian police from the agency led by Crimmins, with Rain Crow riding as his segundo. Jumbo called out, "Hey, have you little fellers seen a hundred or so head of cows in your recent travels?" The newcomers to town just stared back at him, puzzled.

Gatewood recognized Longarm in the gathering gloom and called out, "Glad you're here, Longarm. We're all here to meet that shipment of guns due in by train in a few short hours. What's this about cows? Are more cows missing, for God's sake?"

"Not exactly," Longarm replied. "This larger gent, here, is expecting some in from the south. I sort of want to scan their brands, too, when and if they ever get here. How many soldiers do you have with them gatlings aboard the train, Captain?"

Gatewood looked blank. "Soldiers? Aboard the train? What in the hell for? We're worried about wild Indians, not train robbers."

Crimmins must have been a little smarter. He dismounted and sounded almost anxious as he asked Longarm, "Do you think anyone else could even know those guns are on their way, Longarm? Nobody's *supposed* to know about it but B.I.A. and War. They just wired us today the guns were coming."

Longarm nodded soberly. "Sure. Across open prairie with at least one pair of wire cutters in the hands of someone we *don't* know all that well!"

The agent gasped and almost bleated, "Oh, my God! What are we going to do?"

Gatewood swung his own right leg out of the saddle and snorted, "We don't have to do nothing but wait here for the train, of course. You boys are making mountains out of old-maid worries. The train's coming from the south. The Hostiles who cut the wire for a spell did so to the north

155

and, anyhow, cutting a wire is a lot easier than taking down Morse code for your average unwashed savage!"

He didn't seem to notice how many Indians were in earshot as he opined about Indian brains. He barely seemed to notice his own white troopers as he handed his reins to a dismounted and respectful noncom to growl, "Do something with this horse, Sergeant. Take the rest of your men down by the depot and have 'em cover the arrival of the train. I'll join you when it's due in."

Nobody argued with the officer, so Gatewood as well as Crimmins followed Longarm, the sheriff, and Jumbo back inside. Everyone but Gatewood bellied back against the bar. The captain moved over to a corner table and banged his saber on the floor until the waitress gal brought him his bottle. Longarm grimaced and muttered, "Jesus, she forgot his nipple!"

Crimmins nodded soberly. "You noticed too? Oh, well, at least his *men* are sober and some of his noncoms are old Indian fighters."

Longarm started to ask the agent where his own fighting Indians were. But if Rain Crow and his sidekicks didn't want to drink in a saloon that was crowding up by the minute with whites, it was likely just as well. As other local gents, mostly dressed cow, wandered in out of the dark, more than one mentioned that same scrub herd to Jumbo, who seemed to be getting sullen as well as well lubricated by now. He had just said, "Aw, hell, they ain't coming, and I'm going to spark with my true love!" when a dusty rider nobody in the place seemed to know announced from the batwing doors, "I'm looking for Jumbo Cross!"

"You found him, pilgrim," Jumbo said. "Have you come in peace, or are you just plain tired of living?"

The stranger laughed. "Hold your fire, Slash K. The Triple Eight just sent me to inform you, friendly, that the cows you said you might like to bid on are waiting for you down to the stockyards by the depot."

Jumbo drained his schooner and crashed it down, "It's about time," he said. "How many head are we talking about, and how many have hoof and mouth?"

"Come on down and see for your ownself. You won't find any fixing to either die or win a blue ribbon. Like we told your boss, it's a mixed market herd too cheap to hold during Indian troubles and too expensive to just turn loose."

Everyone started clumping out behind the stranger and Jumbo. Longarm saw Captain Gatewood still sitting there like Little Jack Horner and called out casually, "Don't you want to watch the auction, Captain?"

Gatewood snorted in disgust. "Do I look like a cowboy?" he asked.

It wouldn't have been polite to tell him what he looked like, sucking on that bottle, so Longarm said, "I'd best just go have a look-see at the brands, then. I'll let you know if I spy any big old government initials."

Gatewood didn't answer. He had the neck of the bottle in his mouth. Longarm dropped some coins on the bar in case he never came back alive and went outside. He followed the crowd at a modest distance as they all headed for the railyards. There was something going on here that just didn't smell right. None of the pieces he had to work with seemed too suspicious, studied one at a time. But he'd noticed in the past that when things didn't fit together sensibly, suspicious or innocent, it was generally best to go with suspicious.

By the time he caught up with Jumbo and the others, someone had found the old brand inspector and a railroad lantern. The old man was holding it over the rails to illuminate a wall-eyed calico steer as he observed, "That brand looks mighty recent, boys, and, no offense, it ain't no Triple Eight!"

There was an ominous rumble from the Switchback crowd.

But before it could get really ugly a shadowy figure seated on the fence called out, "Now let's not get too hot, boys! I told you this was a market herd of casually gathered scrub."

"How casually, and offen whomsover?" growled a Switchbacker.

The stranger trying to sell them laughed lightly. "All right, I'll admit some was mavericks when we found 'em on the open range and so we naturally branded 'em to save tedious discussions like we seem to be having anyways. I sure hope nobody here aims to tell me he's never done the same, for I'm too peaceable inclined to call so many grown men liars."

There was a grudging round of lighter laughter from the crowd. The spokesman for the Triple Eight took advantage of it to call out, "Anyone here who's missing stock this summer is welcome to discuss such brands as this herd is being offered for sale with. I'm citing the laws of Montana Territory when I tell you polite it ain't nobody else's business and, if it's all the same with you all, I'd like to start selling this damn beef off. So what am I bid for this fine calico, branded Double Diamond?"

Someone offered two dollars and the argument commenced. Longarm spotted Rain Crow smoking with his back turned to the penned cows and moved down to join him where the crowd was thinner, asking, "See any Interior Department brands in there, Rain Crow?"

The Indian shook his head. "No. I didn't expect to. But how come they wear so many brands if the outfit calls itself the Triple Eight?"

Longarm said, "That ain't mysterious or even too unusual for a shoestring cattle operation. If you want to get into the industry cheap, you file or just squat by good water with plenty of open range around. Then you round up any strays in sight, buy stragglers or cripples off trail herds passing, for the price of their hides, then wait a spell. Given plenty of rest on good grass and water, most runty scrub gets well enough to stagger to the slaughterhouse in time."

"Why do the big outfits let them have the sick cows cheap? Why don't *they* just keep a rest home for sick cows on their own land?"

"Some do. Most don't. It ain't too profitable. The real cost of running a serious spread is the food and wages for your *human* help. A top hand draws too much pay for working a healthy critter from range-dropped calf to side of beef to make it worth his valuable time if he's required to act as a sick nurse, see?"

Rain Crow shrugged. "I liked it better when we ate buffalo. Less complicated. How long do we have to wait here?" he asked.

"Didn't they tell you what time the train was due in with that arms shipment, Rain Crow?"

"Nobody ever tells us anything. The Great White Father treats us as children. Little children. Maybe the blue sleeves know."

Longarm nodded and ambled over to the depot itself where, sure enough, some cavalrymen were seated on the edge of the platform. The sergeant in command said the train was due in about two hours, adding, "Hurry up and wait. They always have us in place the day before anything happens."

Longarm said he remembered his army days that way, too, and went back to get Rain Crow. "I want you to do something sneaky for me," he said. "Do you reckon you could slip you and your own Indian police a quarter mile west, ponies and all, and wait for me there?"

"Easy. What's going on?" Rain Crow asked.

"Nothing but confusion, *here*. So as soon as I get my own mount we'd best look under another shell for the pea!" Longarm said.

He turned away and moved back into town faster than

he'd left it. At the livery he told the boy on duty to help him saddle up the paint pony near the door. The stable boy said, "That's Miss Bonnie's personal mount, sir."

"I know," Longarm said. "I need a good one tonight, and I noticed the other night how good this one was."

The stable hand didn't help him saddle the paint. He went back to get Miss Bonnie's permission. So Longarm had just gotten the paint ready to go when the redhead flew down between the stalls at him, shouting, "You can't ride out on my Pretty Boy, damn it!"

Longarm said, "Sure I can. I'll call him Paint, if you don't mind, and I hope to have him back to you before sunrise. But I can't argue about it now, Red. I got to stop a serious train robbery."

Bonnie might have let it go at that, since she wasn't really stupidly willful, but Jumbo was. He loomed in out of the dark to growl, "Is this little cuss pestering you, Miss Bonnie?"

Longarm sighed. "Damn it, Jumbo, I thought you came into town to buy cows."

Jumbo said, "Didn't like what I saw in the pens. Don't like what I see *here*, neither! Do you want it Fist City style or do you want to fill your fist? It's all the same to me, you bastard!"

Bonnie blanched and cried out, "Jumbo, don't! He's not a bastard. He's the law! He can have my pony. It's all right. We're old friends!"

She shouldn't have said that. Jumbo glared down at Longarm and said flatly, "She ain't allowed to have no friends but *me!* So now I mean to stomp you for certain!"

"Can't it wait till I get back, Jumbo? I really got more serious chores to tend to right now."

Jumbo shook his head and raised his fists. Longarm raised his own, and then kicked the giant in the balls as hard as he could.

160

It almost didn't work. Jumbo was made of sterner stuff than most men Longarm had fought dirty in the past. While he paled and buckled some at the knees, he refused to go down until Longarm sidestepped his rush and pistol-whipped him across the back of the neck. That put Jumbo flat in the straw at Bonnie's feet and, for some reason, she was screaming at both of them. Longarm kicked the giant in the head a couple of times, jumped on his back, and handcuffed his big wrists behind him before he could do half the things he kept groaning that he meant to do if ever he got up again.

As Longarm rose, he placed the key on the sill of the paint's stall, saying, "Don't let him loose until I'm out of here a ways. I mean it. I don't want to kill your true love, Miss Bonnie, but I just don't have time for small-town games with kids."

She must have followed his orders, because nobody seemed to be chasing him as he rode out of town. It only took him a few minutes to find his Indians or, rather, let them find him. He'd sent them west of the tracks because the moon was rising to the east, so when Rain Crow spotted Longarm outlined against the moonlit prairie he called out to him. The white lawman was pleased to see how hard the Indian police were to see against the darkness to the west as he rode in to join them. He asked Rain Crow how many of the boys spoke English and when Rain Crow said all had to, B.I.A. orders, Longarm smiled wolfishly and said, "All right, gents. I'll tell you what's up, because once we're riding we'll be riding too hard for easy conversation, and I don't want any at all. I've just had what you folk call a vision. My medicine may be bad tonight. I could be wrong. But when folks try to razzle-dazzle me I like to look off to the side of the show, not at it. So we're riding down to where *I'd* want to stop a train, away from the madding crowd. The old flag stop hardly anyone uses anymore."

Rain Crow brightened. "Heya! The train *will* stop there, if someone *flags* it!"

Longarm nodded grimly and replied, "That's what I just said. Let's ride, Blackfoot. By midnight you'll either be counting coup or calling me a total fool. But not if we don't get there ahead of that train!"

Chapter 14

The splintered planks of the old rail platform shone like tarnished pewter in the moonlight, save where two men dressed white were standing. One held an unlit railroad lantern down at his side. The other had a red bandanna tied to the muzzle of the Winchester he carried over the crook of his elbow. They both stared down the moonlit tracks to the south. The one with the rifle shifted his weight nervously and muttered, "It's getting late, Ohio. When was you fixing to light that red lantern?"

"When I see the headlight way the hell off, of course," the calmer owlhoot replied. "We're over the skyline from Switchback. But just in case anyone's taking his gal for a prairie buggy ride, let's let 'em *guess* we're here, for now. If you want to be useful, make sure our painted savages is in place over yonder in the grass, Pike."

The rifleman called Pike turned on one boot heel but made no further moves. "They're there," he said. "If I could see anyone they'd be set up wrong. Let's see if I got my own part straight. When they stop for your red light, the engineer will naturally lean out to ask us what in hell's going on. That's when I gun him. What will *you* be doing, Ohio?"

"I told you. I throws this oil-filled lamp against the wheels to give us some light on the subject whilst the others move in, whooping like Sioux, to uncouple the engine and first cars they has the guns in. Then we leaves the survivors here, run the engine and guns up a couple of miles, and unload 'em for our pals to the north. How many times do I have to go over the same ground with you, Pike? We've been planning this payoff move from the very beginning, damn it!"

Pike said, "I know. I still ain't used to playing Injun instead of cowboy. How come you just said we was to yell like Sioux? I thought we was supposed to be Cree?"

"Oh, for God's sake, what difference does it make what kind of wild Indians we are? The idea was to get them to ship them guns and now, by jimmies, they've gone and *done* it, the dumb bastards!"

"I sure hope so. I'm a criminal, not a play actor. Hey, ain't that a headlight coming over the skyline to the south, Ohio?"

Ohio said it sure was, and struck a match to light his false signal.

Farther out in the darkness to the west, Longarm doubted he'd ever have a more tactical time to shoot the bastard, so he lined up his Winchester sights and pulled the trigger as, to his left, Rain Crow shouted, "Heykaya! Kiyiyiyi-yaaaaaaka! and all hell continued to break loose.

Ohio dropped his lantern with a crash and followed it down to sprawl writhing and screaming in the flaming coal oil as it spread out across the dry wooden platform. Pike had meanwhile fired at Longarm's muzzle flash to no avail, since Longarm had crabbed sideways, afoot, to fire the next time, at Pike, from another position. One of the Indian police put a round in him, too, as he sprawled in the burning oil with his sidekick. Nobody on Longarm's side saw fit to put either one of them out of his misery as they twitched like moths caught by a campfire. The Indian police weren't trying to be cruel. They were just too busy shooting at other people outlined by the moon and burning platform. The men trying to aim back at them, invisible against the night save for their muzzle flashes, looked a lot like Indians, too. But hardly any wild Indians ever shouted, "Oh, Christ! I'm gutshot!" or "Jesus, what went wrong?" in English.

Longarm called out, "Hold your fire!" as he saw what had started out as a serious gang of about thirty had been whittled down to less than three still on their feet. But his Blackfeet had themselves a mite worked up. So all of the owlhoots were down and a couple almost scalped before Longarm could calm his men down. It helped when Little Moon rose from the one he'd jumped, holding a feather roach and a full head of hair, braids and all, to shout incredulously, "What's going on here? This one had a *wig* on!"

By this time the train was closer. As the engineer leaned out of the cab, gaping at the eerie firelit scene, Longarm fired his Winchester at the sky and waved the train on. The engineer, no fool, opened the throttle wider and just kept going. There was nothing else to worry about here, now. Longarm and his men went over the rise to where they'd left their ponies and mounted up again.

Rain Crow said, "Heya, that was a good fight. I'm sorry it's all over. It was fun."

Longarm nodded soberly. "It ain't over yet," he said. "We just had us an easy skim of cream back there. I'll let Sheriff Murphy and his boys clean up the mess before it curdles. But from here on the game could get more dangerous than fun."

"Heya, didn't we just get all the Cree raiders, even if they turned out to be crazy white men?"

"They wasn't Cree and they wasn't crazy, Rain Crow. My kind seldom does anything that wild unless it's for money."

"I know. You told us they were going to try to rob that train. But we stopped them. So this time they got no money, right?"

"Wrong. There wasn't all that much money aboard that

train in the first place. They was after enough guns to start a war. A real war . . . no offense. So now I've still got to get the sneaky sons of bitches left, including the master mind."

"How do you know this master mind was not back there with them, Longarm?"

"Easy. They acted dumb. The son of a bitch behind all this flim-flammery has to be smart and sneaky as a wolverine crossed with a snake in the grass."

By the time Longarm led his Blackfoot posse back to town along the tracks the gatling guns and ammo caissons had been unloaded and lined up parade dress in the moonlight. The train that had delivered them was, of course, long gone. The Indian agent, Crimmins, was jawing with the sergeant in charge when Longarm reined in and dismounted near them.

Crimmins asked, "Where on earth have you and my Indians been all this time? We couldn't move these guns out to the agency without them."

"I wouldn't have let the train go on without us if I'd thought you could," Longarm said. "Nobody needs 'em now, and I'm impounding 'em all as evidence." He turned to the noncom. "Where's your commanding officer, Sergeant?" he asked.

The cavalryman looked embarrassed as he replied, "Captain Gatewood's . . . indisposed at the moment, sir."

Longarm nodded. "Well, I was aiming to get everyone important together at the saloon, anyway," he said. "I didn't mean to say you and your men aren't important, Sergeant. But you'd best get these guns out to Fort Banyon for now."

"*All* of them, Deputy? I thought the Indian agency was to have about half."

Longarm shook his head. "War's over. Me and Indian police just won, and there's a hell of a mess to bury to the

166

south. You boys at the fort will get a full copy of my report once I've time to write it up. Meanwhile I want all these dangerous toys under lock and key. Report to your ordinance officer as soon as you get 'em all to Fort Banyon. He'll know what to do."

"What about Captain Gatewood, Deputy?"

"I'll talk to him when and if he sobers up. You got your orders, soldier. Get moving. I got other chores to tend here in Switchback and I can't hardly tend 'em here."

He turned to Rain Crow, still mounted like the other Blackfeet, and said, "We'd best all dismount and move on up the street, sidearms in hand, and leave our critters tethered hereabouts."

Rain Crow swung lightly to earth as he asked, grinning wolfishly, "Do we get to fight some more? I was afraid it was all over!"

Longarm seldom answered foolish questions he didn't have to. He just started walking. Behind him the Indians dismounted, secured their horses, and followed, bemused.

The Indian agent walking at Longarm's side seemed puzzled, too. "Damn it, I wish someone would tell me what's going on around here!" he said. "First the train rolls in, reporting some sort of fire and battle in progress down along the track. Then you show up just as we have our heavy weapons, to tell us we don't *need* heavy weapons, and . . . Where in hell are we going with our fool guns out like this, Longarm?"

"Got to pass the cattle pens to get to the saloon. The other members of the gang might have lit out by now, or they could be laying for us. Either way, that unexpected cattle auction was meant to bring in the serious or casual riders around town, so's their so-called wild Indians would have the moonlit range and the poor defenseless railroad all to themselves."

"Jesus! You say you and my boys jumped wild Indians?"

"Not hardly. I'll explain it all at once to everybody, if we make it up to the bright lights of the big city alive. It's tedious to tell the same tale over and over. Heads up. Them pens ahead look empty now, but you never know."

They were. As Longarm and the others edged in they saw that both the mystery herd and its mysterious herders had departed. Longarm said, "Auction must have gone well. It ain't surprising, at the prices they was asking."

"I didn't stay to see it all," Crimmins said. "But before I moved on to the depot, beef was selling for five dollars a head. Maybe I should have bid on some for my Indians. That's mighty cheap even for scrub, with the price of beef so dear this year."

Longarm grimaced and said, "They could afford to sell it cheap, since they never paid for it in the first place. They wasn't out to make money, here. It was just a flim-flam distraction, like I said. There sure has been a lot of that going on around here of late."

They were met beyond the cattle pens by Sheriff Murphy and half a dozen deputies. "Heard you just rode in with a mess of Indians and a tale to tell, old son," Murphy said.

"I'll shed more light on the subject once we're all enjoying some suds by saloon light," Longarm said. "These Indians are drinking on me tonight, no matter what the law says. At the moment they're all acting as deputy U. S. marshals and, even if they wasn't, they deserve a treat on Uncle Sam."

Crimmins told the sheriff, "Longarm just told me there was something funny about that cattle auction, Sheriff."

Murphy naturally said, "Hot damn! I knowed it was too good to be true! But the rascals just rid out, so if we gathers a posse—"

Longarm cut in to say, "Simmer down. I need you and your jailhouse facilities here, Murph. I know where the rest of the gang is headed. I wired the Mounties to expect 'em.

Me and Crown Sergeant Foster has had interesting discussions on just where the border might be in the past, so he'll get my delicate hint and, to tell the truth, I ain't sure I want any U. S. lawmen meeting up with Mounties where Mounties ain't supposed to *be!* I feel certain that when Foster writes his own report it'll show he rounded them rascals up on the proper side of the border."

Murphy nodded and said, "Good enough. But what about the cows they unloaded on our unsuspecting populace?"

"What the hell, they didn't pay all that much," Longarm said. "So when the government reclaims its beef they can chalk it up to experience."

Crimmins gasped. "Hold on! I'll admit I didn't examine each and every cow by moonlight just now, but there wasn't a government brand on any of the hides I did get to look at."

"He's right," said Murphy. "More than one brand looked suspiciously fresh, but they was all too *small*. I can think of lots of things one might run a big US or ID into, Longarm, but *smaller* ain't one of 'em!"

Longarm said he would explain inside and so, since they'd reached the saloon by then, they all clumped in after him. The place was almost empty now, since most of the men who'd bought mysterious cows that evening had driven them home to join their own herds. Over in the corner, Captain Gatewood hadn't moved. His head was on the table between his hat and his private bottle.

Longarm bellied up to the bar between Crimmins and the sheriff. He was able to meet the eyes of Rain Crow and the others in the mirror behind the bar. He ordered drinks all around on his expense account and waited until he'd rinsed some trail dust out of his mouth before he said, "Well, I ain't got a soap box, but I want everybody to listen tight, because it's sort of complicated."

He saw he had everyone's attention. "Once upon a time

they had a revolution up Canada ways. In fact, it's still going on, and the separatists under Louis Riel are getting skunked. They got numbers and a fancy new flag to fight under, but the government has all the modern weapons. So the Metis chipped in, robbed a few banks and such, and got together the wherewithal to buy themselves some serious guns."

Murphy gasped. "Do you mean to say them fake Cree was really Canadian breeds, Longarm?"

Longarm looked pained. "I wish you wouldn't butt in. I meant no such thing. Neither real Metis nor real Plains Cree have pestered anyone down here. They got enough pestering to do north of the border. The gang raising red in these parts was home-growed crooked Americans who aimed to go into the arms business in a big way, as soon as they could get their scheming hands on said arms. They started staging fake Indian trouble in order to get the B.I.A. and the War Department to do what they just did tonight— send a mess of heavy weaponry and ammo so's the gang could steal it and sell it for a mess of Metis cash on delivery, on the unpatroled stretch of border where the Blackfoot reserve bangs into Canada. The reason the army and the Indian police both had trouble finding the so-called Cree was twofold. In the first place, when they wasn't wearing feathers and paint, they was posing as an innocent cattle outfit on open federal range. The second reason was that everyone, of course, expected to find 'em camped somewhere on the big reserve to the north, closer to their home range. They *hit* from the north most of the time. But then they circled, drove the cows down to the scrub operation, and acted innocent between times."

Murphy objected, "Hold on. Have you forgotten the Indian beef they stole was branded with them big IDs?"

Longarm shook his head morosely. "Nope. They had to

170

shell-game Uncle Sam by shifting cows about under the shells provided by crooked paperwork."

He turned to Crimmins and added soberly, "I want you to keep your mouth shut and listen careful, old son. You got a fine wife who'll likely stand by you, and it ain't as if you actually killed anybody. So if you're willing to turn state's evidence I can put in a good word for you."

Crimmins stared at him, slack-jawed and shaking his head, as if having a bad dream he wanted to awaken from fast. Longarm nodded soberly and said, "I'd best spell out some of the mistakes you made, so as to save us a lot of denials. You shouldn't have flipped that telegraph switch in your cellar that cut Switchback off from Fort MacLeod until, with me looking over your shoulder, you decided it wasn't worth the risk. It was dumb to begin with. We had nothing to say to the Mounties that early. But anyone could see that if the wire wasn't down on the open prairie the connection had to be broken *indoors,* and the only place the wire *went* indoors after leaving the Western Union here was by way of your agency. I wondered how come a lone Western Union crew could have so little trouble with Indians on the warpath who seemed up to tangling with a bigger bunch of Blackfoot, too. But let's get to your even bigger mistake. I checked you out with the B.I.A. You're a senior agent with considerable savvy. A *good* agent, save for feeling underpaid, I reckon. Yet, with Hostiles all around your agency, your own Indian police unable to cope with it, you left your *wife,* the wife I'm sure you're fond of, *alone* and *unguarded* in a frame house miles from help. Nobody with a lick of sense would leave any woman in a situation like that, old son. You know damn well that at the first sign of trouble dependents is evacuated."

Crimmins gulped and said weakly, "I told Mary Lou she'd be safer at Fort Banyon. She refused to leave me."

Longarm shook his head and said, "Nice try. I noticed how she bossed you, fetching you coffee and cake every five minutes. The poor sweet gal will likely wait for you and you might not get more'n five at hard for swindling, if you'd like to come clean total."

Before Crimmins could answer, Longarm pushed him hard, one way, as he spun the other, slapping leather. But the army man who'd been playing possum in the corner still managed to scare the hell out of everyone by putting a round through the mirror behind the bar before Longarm had blown him away from the table with a .44-40 round in the chest.

As glass tinkled to the floor behind him, Longarm muttered, "Hold the agent, Murphy" as he strode forward through the drifting gunsmoke to see how the captain was feeling right now.

Gatewood was seated upright in the corner behind the overturned table, eyes already glazing as he stared blankly up at Longarm with the blood pulsing out of the hole just above his heart.

"Didn't you know I was keeping an eye on you in the mirror, Captain?" Longarm asked. "You'd just *heard* me tell Crimmins I checked *him* out with the B.I.A. You might have known I'd wired the War Department about *you*. You've never had a drinking problem. You've always been a fine soldier. I reckon, with your retirement coming up, and you still only a captain, the chance to make some real money was just too tempting, right? I'm sure sorry it had to end this way, Gatewood. They said you *earned* that decoration at Cold Harbor that time."

Gatewood murmured, "Medals don't pay an old man's way enough to matter. Am I under civilian or military arrest?"

Longarm said, "Neither" as the captain slid sideways to rest his dead gray head on the floor. The tall deputy meant it when he said, "I wish I'd been wrong about you, old timer." Then he turned, walked back to where Murphy was holding Crimmins gently but firmly by one arm, and said, "Let's wrap it up here in Switchback. Since you'll have to reclaim the government beef sooner or later, Murph, the way they worked that part of the flim-flam goes like this. Crimmins here bought lawsome beef to replace the beef he reported stolen. Then he just had his pals rebrand the cows branded with them big IDs and..."

"Rebrand 'em with *what?*" Murphy protested. "It's nigh impossible to run that big brand."

Longarm said, "Hush up and pay attention. They never *run* the government brands. They just branded a big ID right over the old ID to make it look as if the original stolen cows was replaced by *fresh* branded ones. Then they changed the brands of the real replacements just enough so the original owners wouldn't wonder why they was buying their own critters back, and..."

Murphy gasped and said, "My God, I see how it could work! But hold on, Longarm. If the boys just bid on beef they'd sold earlier, for more, how come they don't get to keep 'em? They was never stolen in the first damn place!"

Longarm nodded, "They may not have been stolen, but the B.I.A. *paid* for 'em. This rascal never bought 'em with his own money. So *all* the cows is now the lawsome property of the Blackfoot Nation. But we don't have to sort that out tonight. I'd like you to put Crimmins in your jailhouse for me, for now, and I'll wire Fort Banyon about the captain in the corner. He's no use to Justice any more, and the army may want to bury him decent for old times' sake."

He turned to Rain Crow. "You come with me. Alone. I got other fish to fry with you in private, and you may as well walk me over to the Western Union."

As the two of them left, Rain Crow asked, "If our agent

is under arrest, who's in charge out there now? Snake Killer?"

"I'm afraid they'll send you another white man to guide your primitive footsteps, old son," Longarm said. "But you're still the *law* out there, and we've still got the delicate matter of them scalped and murdered cherry pickers."

"Heya, that is true! But you just said Crimmins and the fake Cree had nothing to do with killing anyone, Longarm!"

"Well, they meant to kill at least me and a railroad crew. So let's not feel *too* sorry for anyone but poor Mary Lou Crimmins. I ain't up to bringing her the news myself, but she'll surely hear about it and come running to the jailhouse with coffee and cake in the near future. As for the two wives of Fish Head and his nephew, Fish Head done it. I'll leave it up to you and the tribal elders as to what you want to *do* about it. Domestic troubles are a pain in the ass even when *white* folks go crazy, so I'd just as soon pass on Fish Head's personal tragedy."

Rain Crow frowned and said, "Thanks a lot! How am I supposed to prove such a crazy charge to the elders, even if it happened?"

"It happened. Add it up. Two gals stuck with an old man go cherry picking with a young stud when there ain't no cherries worth mention left. Old man wonders how come, too, and trails 'em up to their love nest in the bushes. He does what most jealous and betrayed husbands tend to do at such times, then calms down enough to see he'd best cover his tracks."

Longarm paused to light a smoke in front of the Western Union before he added, "Fish Head covered his tracks too good. There were no others leading anywhere but up and down that same path. If there had been, you sharp-eyed cusses would have found them and, if *you* hadn't, *I* would have. So it had to be someone from your settlement, and who else is left? Them sassy squaws weren't hanging horns on any *other* poor old Blackfoot, were they?"

174

Rain Crow sighed. "No. Running Rabbit had an eye for the girls, but I don't think any of them were as fond of him as his young aunts by marriage. I will tell Snake Killer. He and the other elders may punish Fish Head, or maybe let him count coup. Fooling with your uncle's wives is a very bad thing to do."

Longarm said, "That's why I figure I'd best let you folk settle the matter amongst yourselves. I got to go on in and send me a mess of wires now. If I don't see you again before I leave, it was nice working with you again, Rain Crow."

The Blackfoot held out his hand and smiled boyishly. "I like working with you, too, Longarm. Every time we go after someone we get him, and it's always so much *fun!*"

So they parted friendly, and it only took Longarm half an hour or so to inform everyone who needed informing that he'd cracked the case and that he'd be arriving in Denver shortly with his surviving prisoner.

Back outside, he stared morosely up the street at the few lights still burning at this hour. Rain Crow had been right about the fun part being over. It was tidying up after a case that he found such an unrewarding chore. But it came with the job.

He headed for where he had left Bonnie's paint near the depot. As he passed the mouth of a dark alley someone hissed at him from the dark and growled, "Get in here, damn it! We got private matters to discuss!"

Walking into a dark alley late at night was not something Longarm liked to do even when nobody seemed to be up it. Walking into a dark alley occupied by Jumbo Cross seemed downright silly. So Longarm said, "You'd best come out here where I can see you, Jumbo."

The invisible giant sobbed, "I can't! Not with my hands cuffed agint me like this! I ain't as popular as some in Switchback, for some reason!"

Longarm drew his .44, just in case, and moved into the

gloom with Jumbo. Then he laughed and put his gun away again. "Feeling helpless and unpopular at the same time must be a new experience for you, Jumbo. But how come you still have your hands cuffed behind you like that? You saw me leave the key for your true love."

Jumbo heaved a vast sad sigh and replied, "I ain't sure I'm in love with that redhead no more. She laughed like hell as she dropped the key down the front of her dress. Then, worse yet, she cussed me just awful. She said I was a bully and a fool. I just don't understand what's got into that girl lately. She let me walk her home from the church picnic this spring. But since then she's been treating me mean as hell."

Longarm said, "Well you *are* mean as hell, Jumbo. Turn around and I'll see what I can do. May take a spell. I generally unlock them cuffs with a regular key."

As Longarm reached for his pocketknife Jumbo said, "Hurry up. I got to take a leak so bad by back teeth is floating! I'll never forgive that gal if she makes me wet myself!"

Longarm got to work with his pick blade as he said, trying not to laugh, "Just hold the thought, old son. Hold *still*, too, damn it! Like I said, this won't be easy, even with you holding still."

"I sure don't understand women," Jumbo grumbled.

Longarm tried, swore softly, and changed to another blade, saying, "Welcome to the dumb side of the human race, Jumbo. Them she-males will slicker us every time."

"It sure seems so," sighed Jumbo, moving his fool wrists just as Longarm thought he had it. The shorter lawman swore and Jumbo said, "I'm sorry. It ain't easy holding still when you got to take a leak so bad. I don't know why Miss Bonnie treated me so mean tonight, for I've never done a thing to make her mad at me. I mean, I never got fresh or nothing, and since she let me walk her home that time I've stomped every son of a bitch who might have. You say she treated *you* tricky, too?"

Longarm chuckled dryly. "Not the redhead. Another gal down in Denver. I just wired my office to pick her up, if she's still in town."

"I wish *I* got to arrest mean women. What did that Denver gal do to you, Longarm?"

"Set me up for a killing or two. She was a court stenographer, so I doubt she draws more pay than me or my boss. She was the only one aside from us who could have heard when an outlaw mentioned unrecovered holdup loot. She told one of her real boy friends about it, not too long after she kissed me fondly goodbye, I fear. That'll learn me to hang about a gal's neighborhood longer than I have to, after. Hold still. I got the pick on the tumbler and . . . Damn it, Jumbo!"

"I'm sorry. Who was this other gal *really* playing slap and tickle with?"

"Someone named Smith or Jones, I reckon. Knowing she'd be likely to take down a jailed sidekick's word, they must have approached her ahead of us with a better offer. Anyway, since they knew my boss would be staying in Denver but that I was headed north, they decided to bushwhack me before I could drop by Middle Fork and look for the loot, the poor dumb bastards. They weren't as aware of the advantages of telegraphy as the smarter crooks in these parts. But they sure threw me off a mite on what would otherwise have been an easier investigation, and . . . Hold it, I think I got it, and . . . There you go. It's only fair to warn you that if you swing at me again I'll gun you. I've had a long, hard day, Jumbo."

But the giant seemed more interested at the moment in pissing at least a quart against the nearest wall as he gasped,

"Oh, Jesus, that feels good! That mean little redhead sure treated me cruel tonight, and I'll never forgive her!"

Longarm put the cuffs away as he said, "Don't go beating her up, though. You've made enough enemies hitting *men* around here, even if her uncle wasn't the sheriff."

Jumbo sighed and started buttoning his pants again. "I know it ain't right to hit women. But I sure have to do *something* to pay her back, damn her hide!"

Longarm said, "Why don't you try ignoring her? There's nothing that riles a she-male like being ignored."

Jumbo thought for a moment. "You're right. From now on I ain't going nowheres near that sassy little gal. Not even to save her from the advances of less handsome men. *That* ought to larn her to treat me mean!"

Then he turned, stared down at Longarm with a puzzled frown, and asked, "Say, don't I still owe you a kick in the balls, you little rascal?"

Longarm shook his head and said flatly, "I told you I was tired of playing kid games with you, Jumbo. If you don't grow up sudden, some less agreeable cuss is sure to add you to his rep. But I already got me a rep, so you'd best go home now, hear?"

"Shoot, I'll bet I can lick you fair and square, now that I knows you fight dirty."

Longarm showed him how wrong he was by materializing a .44 under his nose, cocked, and saying, as the giant paled, "Growed men don't fight schoolboy style with anything as big as you, Jumbo. Like I said, you're going to get blowed away if you don't start acting sensible. So what's it going to be?"

Jumbo sighed. "I reckon the safest thing to say to you right now would be *adios,* Longarm!"

So Longarm waited until the giant walked away, not looking back, before he grimaced, reholstered his gun, and moved on the way he'd been going.

He found the paint where he'd left it. The Indian ponies had, of course, left with their riders. Longarm said, "I'm sorry to find you so lonesome, Pretty Boy. But I'll take you home now."

He'd just remounted when another rider came down the main drag at him, calling out his name. He reined in and waited. It was one of Sheriff Murphy's deputies. The town lawman said, "I been looking for you. The sheriff says to tell you he's got your prisoner under lock and key and that he's fixing to ride out to the agency so's the rascal's wife can say goodbye to him afore the morning train pulls out with you both aboard her. Murph wants to know if we should arrest that sneaky French Canadian trader for you whilst we're out there."

Longarm shook his head. "Chambrun ain't done nothing sneaky. He was *treated* sneaky. I checked him out by wire with the B.I.A. a long time ago. Until Crimmins sent for him special, for razzle-dazzle reasons, Chambrun was trading, decent, over in the wild rice country. He is a Metis, but he's a U. S. citizen, too, and all Metis ain't mixed up in that lost cause to the north. None of the real crooks we dealt with down here were Metis or even Canadians. They were just greedy bastards, out to make some money off other folks' troubles. By this time tomorrow the Mounties should have picked up the few who got away. You're holding the only real ringleader for me now, for which I'm much obliged."

The Switchback deputy frowned thoughtfully. "Do tell? In the saloon you told that Indian agent it would go easy on him if he turned state's evidence against the real crooks."

"I was fibbing a mite. I was hoping I could trick Crimmins into taking the captain to prison with him. For until Gatewood got too excited for his own good, I didn't have

179

a shred of solid evidence to arrest him on. I knew Crimmins and the others couldn't have gotten away with shit if the captain hadn't been in on it with them. But while a senior officer leading patrols with *no junior officers* present could be called unusual, and leading his enlisted men and Indian scouts the wrong way could be called dumb, neither could be called a federal offense! Had he not saved the taxpayers considerable expense with that one last unlawful as well as wrong move, we'd have never convicted the son of a bitch!"

The town lawman nodded. "I'll tell the others not to pester that trader, then. How long do you figure the agent will get from the judge, in case his wife asks us when we break the news to her?"

Longarm sighed and said, "Twenty at hard, if he's lucky. But don't tell her just yet. It ain't our job, thank God. I sure wish crooks would consider their innocent kin before they rode the owlhoot trail. But they never do, cuss their hides."

"I've noticed. You reckon she'll wait for him, Long-arm?"

"I sure hope not. He don't deserve it. The bastard had it all, with a loving wife, a tolerable job, and a pension instead of prison waiting just down the pike for him. But that's the way things turn out sometimes. Hell, let me get this pony to bed before we wind up blubbering all over one another like sissies!"

The town deputy rode Longarm as far as the livery, where they parted friendly. It was dark inside. Longarm eased the door open as softly as he could and led the paint to his stall. He murmured, "There you go. I'll just get my saddle and possibles off you, leave the money on that box by the door, and . . ."

It didn't work. Bonnie struck a match and demanded, "Where in hell have you been all this time, you brute?"

He noticed she wasn't wearing near enough to appear in such a public place, even by flickering match light. He gulped and said, "For one thing, I had to get my cuffs back from Jumbo. He said you put the key down the front of your dress. But since you seem to be naked as a jay, it must be somewhere else at the moment, right?"

She laughed. "It's by my bed, waiting for you. I left that bully helpless because I wanted to see you come back in fit condition to enjoy a lady's company. You say you took 'em *off* Jumbo? How'd you manage to do that and still look so pretty, darling?"

He slid the door shut lest late passers-by see him jawing with a naked lady and wonder about his upbringing. "Me and Jumbo have an understanding, Bonnie. I don't expect he'll be bothering you no more," he told her.

The match burned down to her fingers. She shook it out and purred in the darkness, "Good. Come on back and bother me yourself, then. For I sure need bothering right now!"

He stayed put and silent. Bonnie groped her way to him in the dark, wrapped her soft bare arms around him, and rubbed her bare body against his rough tweed as she asked, "What's the matter? Has the cat got your tongue?"

He sighed and said, "That ain't my tongue you're rubbing your privates against, Red. I sure wish you'd stop. For I've less pleasing but more important matters on my mind right now."

"What could be more important than screwing?" she demanded. "Have you already met another gal as sweet as me in these parts?"

He cupped a naked buttock fondly in each palm as he held her closer and perhaps more reassuringly, saying, "Ain't nobody got sweeter parts than you around here, Red. The only other woman I have on my mind is fixing to be mad

181

as hell at me now, for I'm taking her husband off to stand trial on awesome federal charges once the next southbound train gets here. So, about what I owe you for the hire of your horseflesh..."

"Screw my horseflesh!" she cut in, adding with a bump and giggle, "Or, better yet, come home to mama and screw *her* flesh instead! God only knows when you'll be up this way again and, you might have noticed, I'm a warm-natured widow woman who just can't get enough when you *are* in town!"

He didn't answer. For though the parts of him she was rubbing her more scandalous parts against knew all too well what they wanted him to say, his brain wasn't sure it could trust the rest of him, and he'd just wired Billy Vail the timetable he intended, or had intended, to follow in delivering his prisoner.

Bonnie reached down between them to unbutton his fly, crooning, "Oh, is all this for little old me?" as she stood tiptoe in an awkward attempt to get it in her, standing.

He laughed and said, "You and me ain't built enough alike to do it that way. Suffering snakes, I see we *are!* But, look here, Red, I still got an early train to catch, and..."

"What time's your fool train?" she cut in, hooking one thigh over his pistol grips to slide more of her lush interior aboard his runaway erection.

He sighed. "You're right. This'd make a lot more sense flat out in bed. But, damn it all, I wasn't planning on going to bed at all before the 5:00 A.M. southbound! I've had a hard day, even before you got me hard, I mean, and it hurts more to get up after a short spell of shuteye than it does to just stay up in the first place."

She slid off him, took the matter firmly in hand, and proceeded to lead him back to her quarters as she said, "You ain't had nothing half as hard today as I mean to get this

182

sweet love tool for us both, lover. As for your fool train, it won't be coming for at least three or four hours. So we've plenty of time for more joyous coming, the right way, in bed!"

He let her lead him to his delightful doom, but protested, "Seriously, Red, there won't be another southbound train until late in the afternoon, and I wired my office I'd be catching that earlier one. So I could get in real trouble if I oversleep!"

Bonnie gave his raging erection a loving squeeze as she demurely replied, "You're already in real trouble if you think I mean to let you fall *asleep* on me this side of sunrise, you sweet, loving rascal!"

Watch for

LONGARM ON THE SANTA CRUZ

seventy-eighth novel in the bold
LONGARM series from Jove

coming in June!

LONGARM

Explore the exciting Old West with
one of the men who made it wild!